THE GROTTO OF TIBERIUS

The Mediterranean island that Michael
Forbes is considering for his father's tourist
agency looks peaceful enough, and even the
evil tales of the Grotto of Tiberius, haunted
by a Roman tragedy, seem just fanciful
peasant superstition and not sufficient to
bring in the tourist trade. However, when
Michael, a stubborn young Yorkshireman,
falls in love with the bright-haired Cristina,
he begins to recognise the force of island
feuds and superstitions. The local magnate,
Sabastian, has sworn to marry Cristina –
even if it means sending a man to certain
death in the Grotto of Tiberius...

THE GROTTO OF TIBERIUS

THE GROTTO OF TIBERIUS

by

Frederick E. Smith

Dales Large Print Books
Long Preston, North Yorkshire,
BD23 4ND, England.

British Library Cataloguing in Publication Data.

Smith, Frederick E.
    The grotto of Tiberius.

    A catalogue record of this book is
    available from the British Library

    ISBN   978-1-84262-557-6 pbk

First published in Great Britain 1961
by Hodder & Stoughton Ltd.

Copyright © 1961 by Frederick E. Smith

Cover illustration © Richard Clifton-Day by arrangement with
Alison Eldred

The moral right of the author has been asserted

Published in Large Print 2007 by arrangement with
Frederick E. Smith

Dales Large Print is an imprint of Library Magna Books Ltd.

Printed and bound in Great Britain by
T.J. (International) Ltd., Cornwall, PL28 8RW

TO MY LATE UNCLE
HAROLD WILSON

CHAPTER 1

From the ship the island floated like a hot summer image in the blue Mediterranean. Dome-shaped, panelled in vineyards, it sloped gently down to the small harbour where bleached, terraced houses gleamed white in the sunlight.

Two men were leaning against the ship's rail watching it. One, Jack Wilkinson, a middle-aged balding man, was sharing his attention between it and the pipe in his mouth which was drawing badly. His companion, Michael Forbes, was more engrossed. He was a younger man, quiet-spoken, broad-shouldered, with a thatch of dark brown hair. He was not handsome – the bone structure of his face was too dominant – but he had a firm mouth and good eyes, blue and observant with a crinkled hint of humour. At the moment these eyes were held by the island, roving from the harbour where the bleached sails of fishing boats were rinsing out the dazzling light to the south coast where high cliffs hung sheer over the sea. He spoke without turning his gaze.

'Surely this is better than you expected?'

Wilkinson removed the pipe from his mouth. 'I don't think so. Why?'

Michael turned to him in surprise. 'It looks attractive enough to me.'

There were times when Jack Wilkinson's greater knowledge of the Mediterranean gave his voice an undertone of condescension. 'They all look attractive from the sea. They'd have a job to look anything else in this sunlight.'

The anchor rumbled down, throwing white splinters over the glass-smooth blue sea. The motor vessel yawed slightly, then steadied. A moment later the gangway was extended. Circling rowing boats, with their high bow-images of the Saints, made for it like ducks scurrying towards a crust of bread. Wilkinson leaned over the rail and hailed one of them in Italian.

'Hey, you! How much to take me and my friend ashore?'

The boat belonged to a fierce-faced old man in a fisherman's jersey and jeans. 'Five hundred lire, signor. With your luggage.'

'Too much. I'll give you three hundred.'

The fisherman's sun-leathered face grinned up at them. 'The days of the galley slaves are over, signor. But from my price one would not know it. Five hundred lire – the cheapest boat here.'

Wilkinson muttered to himself and stared around for another boat, but by this time they were all clustered around the end of the gangway. 'All right,' he shouted down. 'Get your boat into the queue. But hurry it up.'

Michael had given an involuntary laugh at the old man's spirit and now Wilkinson turned to him. 'Cheeky old devil,' he grunted. 'You usually get that sort of thing when they're getting too much money. But I didn't expect it in an out-of-the-way place like this.'

Michael made no comment and not for the first time Wilkinson felt a burn of resentment. Maybe his ways weren't everyone's ways, but they got results and he damned well wasn't going to change 'em for a twenty-seven-year-old kid. Anyway – and Wilkinson found comfort in the thought – old man Forbes wouldn't have put him in charge of the kid on this trip if he didn't think highly of him... The old man liked bluntness – God knows, he was blunt enough himself. And if it came to that, underneath his 'varsity polish, this kid must be just as blunt and obstinate as his old man if all the rumours he'd heard were true. Certainly he was dour – after a fortnight with a man you expected him to loosen up a bit... What Wilkinson, a natural gossip, would not admit to himself was that he could never understand a man who did not like chatter for its own sake.

Wilkinson stared down at the gangway again. About twenty passengers were jostling down it and disembarking into the boats. Wilkinson nodded at them. 'All salesmen from the mainland, if I'm any judge. I'll bet you don't get many of the islanders making the trip. Too expensive for 'em.'

Michael turned to watch the passengers. Minute warm images of the island were still glowing in his eyes and they further awakened the tiny devil of malice in Wilkinson. He jabbed his pipe at the island as the two of them started for the gangway.

'No, Mike; these far off-shore islands aren't the paradises people think they are. Apart from the poverty – and sometimes that's bad enough – you often find people with ideas and prejudices with a couple of hundred years' mould on 'em... On top of that things happen to people who are cooped up together year after year in the same few square miles. Quarrels and jealousies get magnified out of all proportion. For a poor devil who can't fight back and can't get away life can be pretty grim.'

The old fisherman rose and gave them a grin as they reached his boat. '*Buona sera, signori.* Welcome to Veronia.'

His hawk-nosed face was seamed with a thousand wrinkles, but his body was still lean and supple in his seaman's jersey and blue jeans. He took their suitcases, helped them climb into the boat, and then thrust an oar against the gangway. The high-prowed boat rolled and slid away into the waves.

'You are English, signori? Or American?'

'English,' Wilkinson grunted.

'On holiday, signor?'

'No. On business.'

The island drew slowly nearer. A long jetty protected the harbour on the south side, curving out like a swimmer's arm into the incredibly blue sea. Michael leaned forward.

'Do you get many tourists here?'

The old man grinned, shook his head. 'Tourists, signor! There is nothing here for tourists. They want bright lights, casinos. Here we work.'

'How many hotels have you got?' Wilkinson asked.

The old man's uninhibited laugh boomed out over the water. 'On Veronia? We have two, signor.' He glanced around, jerking his head towards the jetty. 'And if you haven't booked a room you'll be lucky to get in either of them. This is the day the salesmen come.'

Wilkinson threw Michael a look of disgust. Michael shrugged. 'I shouldn't worry. It's only for two nights.' He motioned at the old fisherman. 'Why don't you ask him about a guide? He must know nearly everyone on the island.'

Wilkinson nodded abruptly and turned to the old man. 'We're the representatives of an English tourist agency, travelling round this group of islands to see if any of 'em have anything to offer tourists. We've only got two days here, so we'd like a guide to show us round, preferably one who speaks English and knows something about the English people. Do you know of anybody?'

The jetty, bearded with seaweed and emerald green in the sunlight, glided towards them. The fisherman pulled on an oar, guiding the boat towards a steep flight of stone steps. He turned back to Wilkinson.

'Someone who speaks English ... it is difficult here, signor. I know a girl, but am not sure if she will do it. She is a very reserved girl, you understand.'

'Is her English good?'

'They say it is perfect. Her mother was English and she was over in England for some years.'

'Will you ask her for us? We'll pay her well, of course.'

The old man shipped his oars, reached out and checked the boat as it slid alongside the steps. He winked an eye at Michael. 'I'll ask her, and for your sake, signor, I hope she will agree.'

His grin was infectious. 'What do you mean?' Michael asked.

The old man's great laugh boomed back from the side of the jetty. 'Why, signor? Because she is pretty ... the prettiest girl on the island. *Mamma mia*, the times I have wished myself thirty years younger... A lovely girl, signor, but so unhappy. That is why I am not sure about her.'

Michael stared at him. 'Unhappy?'

The old man's expression had completely changed. His wrinkled face was fierce and his eyes as angry as a winter sky. He seemed about to answer, then, changing his mind, he jumped from the boat and extended a sinewy hand. 'Come, signori – hand me your suitcases. The sooner we reach an hotel the better your chances of getting a room.'

They went up the steps with him and along the jetty, picking their way through the bare-footed, sun-blackened children who buzzed around them like flies.

The girl in the lemon print frock and sandals latched the door of the school and crossed the playground to the cobbled road beyond. She was perhaps twenty-two years of age, slim and shapely and very graceful of movement. Her features were attractive, and she had a mass of thick hair that glowed like rich honey in the sunlight. Yet in spite of these gifts her expression and walk betrayed dejection and unhappiness.

A side street branched off the road, dropping down the hillside in flight after flight of cobbled steps to the waterfront below. The girl turned into it and paused. In the warm noon air the noisy chatter of the town below came to her clearly. Her eyes, however, were

17

on the sea that stretched out before her, a great slab of blue marble veined with jade and mazarine. A ship was cutting a broad arrow through it as it headed for the bay, and for a moment a look of intense longing came into her eyes. Then with a quick, almost fierce, shake of her head she dropped her gaze and hurried down the street.

At first the houses flanking it were mostly well-kept bungalows. The girl descended two flights of steps and was approaching a third when she suddenly stopped dead. For a moment she showed distress. Then she recovered herself and faced the man who had stepped out of an alley before her.

He was a handsome young Italian, sinewy and athletic of build, with crisp black hair and bold features. On another man his expensive clothes might have seemed extravagant, but his arrogant carriage helped him to wear them well. His black eyes held a strange mixture of mockery, defiance and eagerness as he approached the motionless girl.

'*Buona sera,* Cristina.'

The girl acknowledged his greeting icily and tried to pass him. As light-footed as a lynx he stepped in front of her. He made a request in a voice that was both ardent and eager, and for a moment the girl looked almost bewildered. Then her lips tightened and she tried again to pass him. Once more

18

he stepped in front of her, his arms extended pleadingly.

'I've waited over half an hour to see you, *cara*. You can't expect me to let you go as easily as that.'

'Why won't you stop it? Why won't you leave me alone?'

He shrugged. 'You know the reason, *cara*. I've told you often enough.'

The girl's voice was low but intensely passionate. 'You've told me a reason, Sabastian, but it isn't the true one. Let me come by.'

He shook his head mockingly. They faced one another, the darkly-handsome man, the white-faced angry girl. Two housewives carrying shopping baskets passed them. One whispered something to the other and received a titter in return. The sound broke the spell and Sabastian gave a laugh. '*Mamma mia,* it is funny. I, who have never liked the English, think it must be the English in you that attracts me. You're as stubborn as old Mario's mare.'

His hot gaze moved from her rich hair to her face, to her shoulders and down her glossy neck. He muttered something to her and the girl's lips curled. 'Where did you hear that? In the cinema?'

Her scorn was the spark to the powder keg of his emotion. He suddenly caught hold of her and pulled her towards him. 'Don't make fun of me, Tina. I mean everything I say.'

She struggled to free herself. 'Take your hands away. Let me go.'

His dark face was inches from her own. 'Why have you changed so much? What's the matter with you these days?'

'As if you didn't know,' she panted. 'Let me go or I'll shout for help.'

'And who on this island would dare to help you?' he sneered. 'Tell me that.'

'You and your thugs... You're a bully. A *guappo*.'

'Say yes and you can go. You won't regret it, I promise you.'

She tore herself away. Anger overcame her and she threw up a hand and slapped his face. From a nearby verandah a watching woman let out a loud congratulatory laugh. A man standing behind her muttered an imprecation and pulled her inside the bungalow. Sabastian swung round to see who had laughed, then faced Cristina. Under his dark skin his face had paled.

'You dared do that to me... In the street!'

She was trembling now from reaction. 'Let me go. Let me go home.'

For a moment tension was like a thin steel wire, about to snap. Then he stood aside, his voice unsteady. 'Go home, then. Go and remind yourself what your stubbornness has done to your family.' As she ran past him he called after her. 'Go and see the mess your brother has got himself into.'

She halted as if jerked around by a rope. 'Giuseppe! What's happened to him?'

The dark handsome face above her was cruel now, sadistic. 'Go and find out, *cara.*'

She was tight-lipped, as taut as a drawn bow. 'If you have harmed my brother, Sabastian...'

He leaned forward. Every whispered word reached her, clear and distinct in its passion. 'On this island I get what I want, Tina... I always get what I want. Which way I get it is for you to decide. It's your responsibility now, not mine.' With that he turned and walked swiftly away.

CHAPTER 2

Cristina ran from Sabastian down the street. She passed a donkey, labouring up the cobbled steps with two packs of vegetables and a bare-footed boy on its back. The bungalows fell away and shabby tenements closed in, narrowing the streets. Washing hung from some of the windows and garbage lay in the gutters. Buxom women chattering in doorways paused to whisper to one another as she hurried by.

She came out into a large cobbled square. Beyond it lay the harbour where the masts of fishing boats nodded lazily. Near them was a row of stalls under which fishwives were busy gutting a new catch. Although the sun was fierce on the unshaded square a number of people were moving across it, preparing to welcome in the weekly boat from the mainland. Children were there in plenty, and their excited voices mingled with the barking of accompanying dogs.

Behind the square was an unbroken row of bars and shops and it was to one of the shops that Cristina hurried. As she pushed open its door a bell tinkled in the house behind.

The shop was large, and after the brilliant sunlight outside was cool and shadowy. It had a faint fusty smell, however, reminiscent of decay, and although its contents, pieces of boat gear, fishing nets, folded sails, small engines as well as articles of general household use, were spread out so as to give an appearance of plenitude, the empty spaces remaining and the general air of depression told their own story.

Cristina had almost reached the rear door that led into the house before her father, summoned by the bell, shuffled through it. Carlo Delfano was a man of medium height and only in his middle fifties, but his stoop and walk made him appear much older. He had sad liquid eyes that had once been striking but now only looked pathetic in a round, sagging face. His scanty iron grey hair was badly in need of trimming, his black suit showed greenish tinges at the elbows and lapels, and his drooping moustaches, no longer waxed and spirited, added the final touch to his melancholy appearance. Like his shop, Carlo Delfano had known better days, and now lacked both the will and the spirit to fight back.

He gave an exclamation of pleasure at seeing Cristina. 'Hello, *cicci*. You're home a little earlier than usual. Didn't you have to keep any of the little rascals in today?'

She returned his kiss with affection. 'No. For once they all behaved themselves.' As she drew back her tone changed. 'Where's Giuseppe? Is he home for lunch yet?'

'Yes. He came in five minutes ago.'

She searched her father's smiling, worried face. 'Was there anything wrong with him? Did he seem upset?'

Carlo showed his surprise at the question. 'I don't think so. A little quiet, perhaps, but I blamed that on the wine he drank last night. He was out again with those two hooligans Guido and...'

She was at the door. 'Where is he now?'

'Up in his room, I suppose. But what is it, *cicci?* Why are you looking so worried...?'

Cristina ran into the house. Down the passage, through the open kitchen door, she could see her stepmother, Maria. Maria was a tall, strong woman of forty-five, with features that were still handsome but as hard as granite. She had been married to Carlo for three years, having caught him on the rebound after the death of his English wife. In those days, when his business had been flourishing, Carlo had seemed a good catch in spite of having two school-age children. But times had changed and so had Maria's opinion of her luck.

She was bending over the stove when Cristina caught sight of her, and the girl did nothing to attract her attention. Instead she hurried upstairs to Giuseppe's room. She tapped on the door, then opened it a few inches.

'Peppi. Can I come in?'

Her brother was sitting on the edge of his bed. He was a youth with a strong resemblance to her, particularly about the forehead and eyes and in the light colour of his skin. His tousled abundant hair was darker than her own, however, and in his mouth and chin there was a faint reminder of his father. For a boy he had a sensitive face, but his general good looks were marred by a hint of sullenness about his mouth and eyes.

Cristina was careful to close the door behind her before she spoke. 'I've just seen Sabastian, Peppi. And he says you're in some sort of trouble. What's happened?'

The boy's eyes had lightened on seeing her but now they fell away. 'Nothing,' he

24

muttered, rising restlessly from the bed and slouching across to the window. 'At least nothing to make a fuss about.'

Cristina followed him. 'I'm not Maria, you know,' she said quietly. 'You can talk to me.'

For a moment the boy's face softened. 'It's nothing, Tina. Just a bit of fun that went wrong. I'll find the money somehow.'

Cristina's eyes dilated and she caught hold of his arm. 'Money! What have you done?'

Tiny beads of sweat were glistening on the boy's forehead. He turned on her angrily. 'For heaven's sake don't you make a fuss. It'll be bad enough when they hear downstairs. I couldn't help it.' He turned away again and kicked sullenly at the wall below the window. A piece of plaster flaked off, whitening his shoe. 'I was drinking in the piazza last night with Guido and Stephan when a lorry drove up near us. The driver got out and went into a bar for a drink. Guido saw he'd left the ignition key inside and dared me to drive it round the square...'

Her face was pale. 'But you haven't a licence. You can't even drive properly.'

'You don't have to remind me,' he said bitterly. 'Anyway, to cut it short it ended up with my bumping into the sea wall and damaging a new bicycle that was leaning against it. It belonged to old Carmillo – you know, the chap who has the vegetable shop in the Vicolo Roma. He said that for your sake he'd give me three days to find the money before telling the police.'

'How badly was the bicycle damaged?' she asked.

Giuseppe grimaced. 'Oh, it was a complete write-off. I jammed it against the wall.'

The tension built up from her meeting with Sabastian had not yet eased. 'How can you do such mad things when you know the struggle we're having...' Then, seeing she was only driving the boy's shame deeper into him, she checked herself. 'I'm sorry. What about the lorry? Was it badly damaged too?'

'A headlight was smashed,' he muttered. 'And there was a pretty bad dent in one wing. But that's not so important. I found out from the driver that it belongs to Sabastian and I went to see him this morning. He was very decent and told me not to worry about it.'

She drew in her breath sharply. 'Sabastian!' She moved from him as if the room were a cage and she an animal trapped in it. 'Always Sabastian. Those two friends of yours who are always getting you drunk and into trouble – they're both Sabastian's men too, aren't they?'

Giuseppe was immediately on the defensive. 'Don't start all that over again, for heaven's sake. Half the people on the island work for him, one way and the other. You're not suggesting the whole thing was a frame-up, are you?'

'Why not?' she asked fiercely. 'The lorry stopped near you ... the driver conveniently left the ignition key inside... Guido notices it and knows you can't drive properly...' Her expression changed, became frightened. 'What will he do next? You might have killed somebody last night.'

Her suggestion was a harsh abrasive to the boy's pride, darkening his sensitive face. 'Don't talk such rot, Tina. Why should he do such a thing to me? We're quite friendly. Look how he behaved this morning.'

She tried to make him understand. 'Every time he gets us into trouble it makes things harder for me. Surely you can see that. And it's even worse when we get into his debt. We must pay him for the lorry – otherwise it puts me in an impossible position.'

Giuseppe shook his head disbelievingly. 'I can't see why you've got your knife in him so much. He's not a bad chap – he's always been decent enough to me. And look at the money he's got.'

She tried to keep the bitterness from her voice. 'Money isn't everything, Peppi. That's something you've got to learn.'

Giuseppe turned to the window, face sullen and envious as he stared out at the ship in the bay. 'It's everything as far as I'm concerned. Look what it could do for us. We could be somebody again, have decent clothes and a car. And best of all we could get away from this rotten dump and go to Naples or Rome.'

For a second the longing was naked in the girl's eyes again. Then came the quick, fierce shake of her head. 'This isn't getting us anywhere. How much money have you got?'

Giuseppe pulled out his empty trouser pockets. A piece of grey wool floated down to the floor. 'I gave old Carmillo the few lire I had left. I've nothing more until next pay day and then Maria takes most of it.'

He stared hopefully at Cristina. She bit her lip. 'I've only got one thousand seven hundred lire. I don't know where I can get any more...' Her eyes suddenly fell on a small gold watch she wore round her right wrist, a watch left her by her mother. Giuseppe followed her gaze and gave a start. 'No,' he muttered. 'Not that. And anyway it wouldn't bring enough.'

'It would be a help. It's gold... It would be a serious charge, Peppi. You can be imprisoned for driving without a licence.'

The boy's hand was on her wrist, protecting the watch. 'No. Not that...' His voice suddenly thickened. 'I'm sorry, Tina. It was stupid of me. I shouldn't have done it.'

She brushed her cheek against his lowered head. 'You didn't think ... I know that. But we must get the money from somewhere. We shall have to ask Father.'

That had been inevitable from the beginning, but she had put off the moment as long as she could. It wouldn't be so bad if her father lost his temper and shouted at Giuseppe as in the old days. But now he would only shake his head, give a heavy sigh, and somehow look even smaller in his old black suit.

And Maria would have to hear. No matter involving money could be settled without Maria's consent. Cristina swallowed down the cold lump in her throat and put an arm round the boy's shoulders. 'Come on, Peppi. We'd better go and get it over.'

The boy was staring down at the piazza. Cristina followed his eyes and saw a lean stringy figure in a fisherman's jersey and jeans making for the shop. He disappeared beneath them and a moment later the shop bell rang.

Cristina turned to Giuseppe. 'Pietro! I could ask him for help.'

The boy's sensitive face showed contempt. 'What could he lend us? He's poorer than we are.'

'Every lire will help. And I know he'll do everything he can for us.'

At that moment her father called from the bottom of the stairs. 'Tina! Pietro wants to see you.'

Cristina retuned to Giuseppe five minutes later. Her expression was one of renewed

hope and hesitation. 'Pietro says two Englishmen have just arrived on the island.
They want a guide to show them round –
someone who can speak English. Pietro
wants me to do it.'

The boy's eyes showed surprise, then
brightened. 'That's a bit of luck, isn't it?
How much will they pay you?' Then he
noticed her expression. 'What's the matter?
You'll do it, won't you?'

She moved away restlessly. 'I don't know
… I don't want to.'

'What's wrong with it? It's Saturday tomorrow – you're free all day. And if they pay
you enough we mightn't have to ask father…'

Bitterness tinged her eyes. 'Wait here,' she
said quietly, going to the door. 'I'll go and
speak to them.'

He watched her from his window, her
yellow frock swinging alongside the blue
jeans of Pietro as they walked towards the
hotel that stood further along the piazza.
She returned fifteen minutes later and came
straight up to his room. She nodded quietly
in reply to his eager, questioning eyes.

'I've agreed to do it. I start in the morning, at ten o'clock. Pietro is borrowing a car
as they want to see the Grotto first.'

'What are they paying you?'

'Pietro arranged that. Five hundred lire an
hour.'

At first he looked jubilant. Then he

30

frowned. 'It all depends on how long they want you. Did they give you any idea?'

He had to repeat his question. She was thinking of the man who had been lounging on the sea wall at the other side of the piazza the whole time she had been talking to the two Englishmen. She was almost certain he had been one of Sabastian's men.

She shook her head. 'No, but they leave on Sunday afternoon for the other islands. So it can't be for more than a day and a half.'

Giuseppe made a rapid calculation. 'Then we're still going to be short,' he muttered. 'Unless you try to work a rake-off from some of the shopkeepers. It's worth a try.'

She stared at him in astonishment. 'A rake-off? What on earth do you mean?'

'Tell a few of them that you'll bring the Englishmen to their shops if you get a percentage on everything they buy. They're bound to want souvenirs and that sort of thing.'

Her indignation was tempered by shock at this glimpse of the slow corrosion of Sabastian's influence. 'Whoever gives you such ideas? What would Mother have said if she'd heard such things?'

His eyes fell and he turned sullenly away. An ache for him rose like a heavy bruise inside her. At the door she turned. 'Don't say anything to Father yet,' she said quietly. 'Wait until Sunday to see how much I earn.'

Wilkinson came out of the front door of the hotel and approached Michael who was sitting at a table on the covered verandah outside. 'We're eating early – at seven,' he grunted. 'I've just arranged it with the manager.'

Michael nodded. Wilkinson dropped into a chair opposite him and took a swig from his glass of beer. 'It doesn't get much cooler,' he grumbled. 'I'm still melting at the seams.'

Both men had discarded their jackets. The sun was still fierce on the cobbled square before them although the shadows of the buildings on it were lengthening. At that moment it was almost empty. The ship had sailed three hours ago and the fish stalls were closed and still. Wilkinson cocked a suspicious eye at the square and then turned to Michael.

'I don't like the way the manager apologised for giving us a front bedroom. Sounded a bit fishy to me.'

Michael glanced at him. 'I thought he was apologising for only having a double room.'

Wilkinson shook his head. 'No; it isn't that. It's Friday – pay night. And unless I'm mistaken this is the piazza, the place where everyone comes to drink wine and make whoopee. If it is,' and he jerked his head upwards, 'that bedroom up there is going to be a torture chamber in three hours' time.'

Michael grinned. 'We can stick it for a couple of nights.'

Wilkinson gave a doubtful grunt. In the silence that followed a pigeon could be heard, cooing monotonously against the neutral murmur of the sea. Wilkinson took another swig of beer.

'What did you think of the girl? She's a good-looker all right, isn't she?'

Michael's eyes moved quickly on him, turned away. 'Yes, she is. Very attractive.'

'Seems intelligent too. Bit reserved, mind you, as that old pirate of a fisherman said, but we'll soon thaw her out. Hello, who's this?'

A man was approaching the verandah. He was young, dressed in a well-cut linen suit, and darkly handsome. He ran up the three steps that led into the verandah, saw the two men and smiled, showing even white teeth. *'Buona sera, signori.* Are you the two Englishmen who arrived this afternoon?'

Wilkinson stared at him, voice curt. 'Yes. What do you want?'

The man reached into his inside pocket, pulled out a card. 'I would like to introduce myself, signor. My name is Cerone. Sabastian Cerone.'

Wilkinson glanced at the card. His tone was slightly less curt when he looked up again. 'You'd better sit down, Signor Cerone.'

Sabastian dropped easily into a chair. He pulled out a gold cigarette case and offered it to the two men. The cuff of his linen suit fell back, revealing an expensive gold watch. This display of wealth, almost ostentatious in its presentation, did not escape Wilkinson whose tone was now almost civil.

'What can we do for you, Signor Cerone?'

Sabastian's dark face was keen and businesslike. 'I understand you and your colleague are the representatives of an English tourist agency.'

There was nothing wrong with the island's grapevine, Wilkinson thought. He nodded. 'That's right.'

Sabastian leaned forward. 'Then perhaps we can do business, signor. First I must explain that I am a man of some influence on this island – I own a fishing fleet and have interests in most of the other industries. For a long time I have thought this island an ideal place for tourists, but so far few have come. As a result we have only these two hotels, both small and old. But if you were to recommend the island to your agency and send us tourists, I and a few associates would guarantee in turn to build a new and bigger one to make them comfortable. You are following, signor?'

Wilkinson nodded. 'Fair enough. And I'll bear it in mind. But you realise we can't make any promises yet – we haven't had time to look around.'

The Italian threw out his arm expressively. 'What more do you need to see, signor? Here is the sun, the blue sea, the clear sky. To the English in their fog it will seem like heaven.'

Michael was watching the Italian's handsome, mobile face with interest. Until now his keen black eyes had never left Wilkinson's face. Now they shifted to Michael, watchful and assessing. Weighing up their credulity, no doubt. And possibly weighing up their integrity too... Michael wondered with amusement how long it would be before a bribe were offered them.

'That's all very well,' Wilkinson grunted. 'But there are a hundred or so islands in the Mediterranean with blue seas and clear skies. It's got to have more than that to attract tourists these days. But we'll give it a fair look-over – you can assure your friends of that.'

Although his words were clearly meant to end the conversation the Italian did not move, and Michael suddenly had the feeling there was something else he wished to know but would not ask outright. He watched and listened with interest.

'In that case you will need a good guide, signor. Let me provide one for you.'

'We've already got one,' Wilkinson told him. 'A girl who speaks English.'

Sabastian's keen eyes flickered like the

shutter of a camera that had at last found its target. 'A girl, signor? May I ask who?'

'A Miss Delfano. A schoolteacher.'

'I see… You are paying her, signor?'

'Of course we're paying her. We wouldn't ask her to do it for nothing.'

Sabastian nodded, showed polite regret. 'It is a pity I did not meet you earlier, signor. I would have provided you with a guide free of charge. After all you are valuable guests to us. Could you not speak to Miss Delfano and explain?'

Michael's answer was ready as Wilkinson turned to him. 'No, Jack. We've already promised the girl. We can't change our minds now.'

'But it'll save us four or five thousand lire…'

'No; we've made a bargain. I think we ought to stick to it.'

Wilkinson was not over-pleased by what he took to be an adoption of authority. 'All right. I'm only trying to look after your father's money.' He turned back to Sabastian. 'No; my colleague here doesn't think it would be fair to the girl. So perhaps we'd better leave things as they are.'

There was a stiffness in the smile Sabastian gave to Michael. 'Perhaps I should explain, signor – these islands are not like England … here women do not take on this kind of work with strangers. Please do not misunderstand me – I have the greatest respect for Miss Delfano: in fact we grew up as children together. For her sake as much as anything I advise you to have a man for a guide.'

Michael's voice was as dour as his rugged face. 'Miss Delfano must know all this, and if she accepts the work then, as I see it, it is nobody's business but her own.' He stamped out his cigarette and pushed back his chair. 'You'll have to excuse me now – I have to wash before dinner. Coming, Jack?'

Wilkinson hesitated, then also rose. 'I suppose I'd better.' He held out his hand to the Italian. 'Nice meeting you, signor. If you come and see us before we leave we'll give you our views of the island.'

There was a thinness about Sabastian's smile as he shook hands with Michael. When he had gone Wilkinson turned to the younger man. 'You were a bit short with him, weren't you? It's probably quite true what he said about the woman – I told you these islanders were a pretty prejudiced lot.'

Michael turned away without answering him. Wilkinson gave a shrug and followed him into the hotel.

CHAPTER 3

Michael leaned against the rail of the bedroom balcony, watching the piazza below. It
was late evening and the huge cobbled
square was throbbing with life. Young people
paraded across it, boys eyeing girls, girls
giggling their pleasure and darting swift,
bold glances in return. Crowded tables
littered the piazza in front of the hotel and
paraffin-lit stalls, erected after sundown,
peddled their wares around its perimeter.
Noise rose to the balcony like the heat from
a hundred small fires: from a portable radio
playing Neapolitan dance music, from a
party of drunks playing dice on a wine-
stained table, from a group of teenagers
singing around a bearded guitarist. All the
vitality of the town, at rest during the hot
afternoon, seemed to have been sucked into
the piazza that evening, and it bubbled and
seethed like a great hotchpot.

The door behind Michael opened and
Wilkinson came out on the balcony in his
shirtsleeves. He stared down at the piazza in
disgust.

'Nearly eleven and look at 'em,' he
grunted. 'I'll bet you they'll keep it up until

well after midnight.'

Michael nodded. 'I thought I'd take a walk until things quieten down a bit. Feel like coming?'

Wilkinson grimaced down at his feet. 'Not again. That walk we had earlier on round the town finished me. I'll get a book and read for a while.'

Michael nodded, threw on his jacket, and went downstairs. At the foot of the verandah steps he turned left, threading his way through the crowded tables. In front of him a pavement artist worked with coloured chalks in the light of two paraffin lamps. Michael studied the pictures a moment and then walked on, jostled by the crowd. A beggar thrust a tin cup under his nose. 'A gift, signor. A gift for the Saints...'

He dropped a coin in the cup. Thirty yards more and he reached a row of brightly-lit stalls. He passed between two of them into the darkness beyond. Here the piazza narrowed into a waterfront, flanked by old picturesque houses. A half-moon floated over them, throwing jet black shadows on the silvered cobbles. As he walked the noise of the piazza gradually merged into the low swish of the sea.

He was crossing the dense shadow of an old warehouse when he saw the distant figure of a girl approaching him. She was walking slowly as if deep in thought, but something familiar in her graceful movements made his heartbeats quicken. He paused, watching her. She crossed a moonlit strip of waterfront, turned her head, and then halted sharply, facing the silent warehouses. Michael saw a lighted cigarette first, glowing like a firefly in a doorway, before he noticed the dark shadow of a man. To his surprise the girl spoke first, her voice sharp and angry. The man said something in return, following it with a low, mocking laugh.

The girl's repose had disappeared now and she walked quickly away along the waterfront towards Michael. The man in the doorway did not move in pursuit until she was thirty yards or more from him, then he sauntered out after her, hands in his pockets and cigarette in his mouth. Michael could see now that he was wearing an open-necked shirt of some dark material and was slimly-built with sleek, black hair.

The girl noticed Michael now and paused as though trapped. Seeing her fear Michael stepped out quickly into the moonlight. 'Hello, Miss Delfano. I'm sorry – I hope I haven't frightened you.'

Her voice was slightly breathless. 'Mr Forbes ... no, it's all right. I didn't see you at first, that was all...'

The man behind her had stopped and was watching them. Michael motioned at him. 'I couldn't help noticing what happened... Is he bothering you? Would you like me to have a word with him?'

Her reply was quick, alarmed. 'Oh, no. Please don't do anything...' As though to draw him away she began walking on towards the town.

Michael fell in alongside her. 'Have you been for a walk?'

'Yes. It was so noisy in the piazza – I knew I wouldn't be able to sleep...'

He made his tone light in an effort to relax her. 'Are Friday nights always like this? Our room is right over the piazza and the noise is quite something.'

She gave him a quick, anxious smile. 'I'm afraid they are. The fishermen are paid on a Friday.'

They walked in silence for a moment. The man behind them had disappeared into the shadows and Michael turned his attention back to Cristina. She interested him, not only because she was attractive, but because of the reserve that seemed to make her almost morbidly afraid to be seen talking to strangers. He had noticed in that afternoon on the verandah of the hotel – her apprehensive glances at everyone that passed by. He saw it now – the paleness of her face and the way her eyes anxiously probed the shadows of the passing houses.

Yet, remembering Wilkinson's comments on the island, he realised the explanation could be a simple one. Pausing, he turned to her. 'It's just occurred to me that I'm not in England now and I may be out of order in walking along with you in this way. If I am, please tell me. I shan't be offended, I promise you.'

Her hesitation made him certain she was going to accept the escape route offered her. Instead the delicate muscles of her face tightened as though in defiance. 'It isn't an offence, Mr Forbes. I'm grateful for your company.'

The graciousness of her reply made him warm towards her. A moment later they reached the edge of the piazza. Its lights and noise reached out like drunken arms, trying to pull them to its wine-soaked, lusty body. To the left the silent jetty lay quiet in the moonlight. Michael motioned to it. 'I think I'll take a walk down it before turning in. Will you come with me?'

Once again she hesitated but only briefly. 'Very well. But only for a few minutes.'

He had a feeling of elation as they followed the sea wall that ran behind the stalls. The noise faded behind them as the jetty led them out to sea. They passed half a dozen darkened, empty stalls. The moonlit water in the harbour rose and fell like the breast of a sleeping woman. On their left shallow waves broke against the black rocks like quicksilver.

There was a bench at the end of the jetty . Before she sat down Michael noticed the anxious glance she threw back along the silent jetty. He was curious to learn more about her, but instinct told him it was better first to draw questions from her.

He offered her a cigarette. She refused it but insisted he smoked himself. He inhaled deeply and settled back on the bench with a sigh of contentment.

'If it were all like this I wouldn't mind this job at all. Unfortunately it isn't.'

Her eyes left the sea and rested on his face shyly. 'You don't like your work?'

'No. I'm not at all keen on bringing hordes of tourists down on places like this. But it's my father's business and he's been trying to get me into it for years. You know how fathers are – the ambitions they have for their sons. This time I've promised to give it a try.'

Her eyes remained on his face. 'You haven't always done this work, then?'

'No. After university I had two years in the Army in Malaya, and when I got back I found I couldn't settle in an office. So for another two years I've been roaming about doing odd jobs under Father's constant dis-approval.' Without knowing it his voice became moody and curt. 'We're both York-shiremen and both pretty pig-headed, I sup-pose. Anyway, to cut the story short, six months ago he gave me an ultimatum –

either to get right in or to get right out. So to please him I made a big effort and here I am.'

She nodded sympathetically. 'I see. How do you come to speak Italian so well?'

He smiled ruefully. 'Father again. Italy was always his firm's happiest hunting ground, and as he'd already decided when I was a kid at school that I was going into his business, he made certain I was taught Italian instead of the usual French or German. That's why I'm out here now – learning all about Italy before settling down for the rest of my life in his Leeds office.'

Confidence was growing between them like a tenuous invisible bridge. Sensing it he turned to her. 'You said this afternoon that your mother was English. How did she come to live out here?'

'A long time ago my father had to go to England on business. He met my mother at the tea party given by one of the businessmen. He fell in love with her on sight and would not leave England until she had agreed to marry him.'

He laughed. 'Your father must have been a tenacious man.'

Humour rang like a tiny bell in her voice. 'Yes. I think he was in those days.'

'So you were born here?'

'Yes. Both my brother and I.'

'But you said this afternoon that you had gone to an English school.'

'Yes. My mother sent me to a boarding school when I was twelve. She never said anything, but I think she found the island too provincial and wanted us to have a more liberal upbringing.'

'She wasn't too happy here, then?'

'Oh; I don't think she was unhappy. She and father were devoted to one another. I think it was just that she didn't want Giuseppe and me to grow up too prejudiced, that was all. Of course Father could afford to send us in those days. Things were different then.'

'Business is bad now?' Michael asked sympathetically.

There was no self-pity in her. The words had slipped out and her expression showed she regretted them. 'It isn't as good as it was, no.'

He did not pursue the point. 'And now you are a teacher? When did you come back to the island?'

'Four years ago, when my mother died. Giuseppe hadn't yet gone to England – he never did go, as things turned out – and I couldn't leave my father alone to look after him.' She turned to Michael with a naïve truthfulness that he found irresistible. 'I hope Pietro didn't tell you I was a qualified teacher – I was far too young to go to training college before mother died. But they have difficulty in getting teachers to come to these islands, and one doesn't need to be qualified to teach in the junior and infants' school.'

Pietro had made it sound as if she were the Minister of Education – not that it mattered. 'We're very grateful to Pietro,' Michael told her. 'He couldn't have found us a more charming guide.'

She looked quickly away and did not answer. Across the bay to the south cliffs rose black and sheer from the moonlit water. Michael motioned to them. 'The Grotto of Tiberius is over there, isn't it?' When she nodded he went on: 'My colleague is hoping it might be the attraction needed to bring tourists here. How did it get its name and what is the true legend behind it? I've heard at least half a dozen versions and they've all been different.'

Cristina was staring across the moonlit bay. When she spoke her voice was low. 'The legend is a very sad one. The Grotto is supposed to be haunted by two lovers and their murderers…'

'Haunted?' he interrupted with interest.

'Yes. According to legend Tiberius lived for a while on this island. He is supposed to have been attracted by a very beautiful girl only a few days before the girl was due to marry. Tiberius stopped the marriage and told the lovers never to see or speak to one another again under pain of death. But they loved one another too much to obey, and because the girl was always being watched the only place they could meet was in the Grotto. They used to go singly, at night, and return before the dawn. But one day someone on the island betrayed them to Tiberius. In his fury he sent a boat containing six of his best swimmers to the Grotto on a night when he knew the lovers were meeting there. The swimmers dived into the sea, swam underwater into the Grotto, dragged the lovers down from the rocks, and held them under water until they were dead. Since that day the Grotto is supposed to be haunted. The churning of the sea is supposed to represent the death struggles of the lovers and the sobbing sound is their cry of fear.'

'Sobbing sound?' Michael asked, fascinated.

A shudder ran through the girl, as if a sudden draught had stolen on them from the warm night. 'Yes. At certain times the sea becomes terribly rough around the Grotto and a loud sobbing noise comes from it. I've never seen or heard it myself, but nearly everyone on the island believes the Grotto is evil and won't go near it.'

'Do you believe these things happen?'

She hesitated. 'I find it hard to believe the Grotto is haunted but I do feel these things might happen. There have been so many reports right down through the ages, and many fishermen have been killed.'

Her voice broke off and Michael saw she was staring at something down the jetty. Turning quickly he saw a shadow disappearing into the darkness of the stalls. As he turned back to Cristina she rose, the nervous haunted expression back on her face.

'I must be going now. Please don't bother to come with me…'

He was already on his feet and he started along the jetty with her. As they reached the stalls she kept her eyes averted but Michael saw the man, standing in a shadowy gap between two of them. Without a word to Cristina he turned abruptly and made straight for him, ignoring her sharp cry of protest.

'What's your game? Why are you following us like this?'

Startled, the man had stepped back, his hand leaping to his hip pocket. He recovered quickly and shrugged his thin shoulders. 'The jetty is for all, signor. Others can enjoy a walk in the moonlight too.'

'You were following us. Why?'

The man's features were not distinct in the shadows, but he had a small, cat-like head, narrow eyes, and greased-down black hair. His breath smelt strongly of garlic.

'A cat can look at a king. It is no crime, signor.'

Cristina was pulling at Michael's arm. 'Leave him alone, please. Don't argue with him.'

Michael's face was dour, his voice as blunt as a clenched fist. 'You haven't answered my question. Why are you following us?'

The man shrugged and nodded mockingly at Cristina. 'Why don't you ask her, signor? She knows better than I. I only do as I'm told.'

Confirmation of his suspicions that there was some mystery surrounding the girl made Michael turn towards her. She pulled his arm frantically. 'Come away, please. I want you to come.'

Seeing she was near to tears he allowed her to lead him away after throwing a last, threatening glance at the thin Italian. They crossed the piazza and came to a side passage that led to the house behind the shop. At its entrance Cristina turned to him.

'Can you get someone else for tomorrow? Please don't think badly of me, but I think now it would be better if I don't come.'

'Why not? Because of public opinion?'

She stared at him. 'Public opinion? Oh, no; it isn't that.'

'Then it has something to do with that man who was following you tonight. What is it? Will you tell me?'

For the briefest of moments she hesitated. Then she gave a quick, fierce shake of her head. 'No. It can't do any good... Please don't ask me.'

He was as stubborn as the grey moorland

rocks of his homeland. 'If you don't want to tell me, that's your own business. But I still want to see you tomorrow.'

The glow from the piazza lit up the indecision on her face. Her low-spoken words, almost drowned by the noise around them, were addressed only to herself but added to his already intense curiosity. 'I know you've no time to find anyone else. And it is only for two days – surely that cannot cause trouble...' Her face rose, as did her voice. 'Very well. I'll come as arranged.'

Questions rose involuntarily into his relieved eyes. She saw them and turned quickly away. 'Tomorrow morning, at ten o'clock. *Arrivederci.*'

'*Arrivederci,*' he said slowly, watching her vanish down the dark passageway.

CHAPTER 4

The following morning Pietro, the old fisherman, called at the hotel. As Wilkinson had not yet finished his breakfast Michael went out into the hall to see him.

The old man, lanky in a blue shirt, jeans, and heavy sea boots, was staring down at a magazine on the hall table. His fierce blue eyes lifted the moment Michael appeared and recognised him at once.

'*Buon giorno, signor.*'

'Hello. Have you come about the car?'

The old man handed Michael a slip of paper. '*Si, signor.* All is arranged. You go to this address at nine-thirty and the car will be waiting for you.'

'How much do they want for it?'

'A thousand lire until noon, two thousand lire for the full day.'

He ought to haggle, Michael knew, but in fact it was considerably less than he had expected to pay. 'Whom do I give the money to?' he asked.

Pietro's blue eyes twinkled wickedly. 'Old Martello might be embarrassed to take money from an Englishman, signor. To spare his feelings you can pay me, signor, and I will pass it on to him.'

Michael laughed. 'All right. When do you want it? In advance?'

'No. You pay me when you have finished with the car. If you do not see me around, do not worry – I will call at the hotel this evening. You know the time Signorina Delfano is coming round?'

'Yes. Ten o'clock.'

As the old fisherman turned to leave Michael had a sudden thought. He motioned to the small lounge on the right that was deserted. 'Will you stay a few minutes? There's something I'd like to ask you.'

51

Pietro clumped into the lounge and sat awkwardly at one of the tables.

'Will you have a cup of coffee?' Michael asked.

The old man shook his head. His keen eyes searched Michael's face. 'What can I do for you, signor?'

Michael lit a cigarette to cover his embarrassment. 'It's about Miss Delfano. From what you said yesterday I gathered you knew her very well.'

Under his bushy eyebrows the old fisherman's eyes were intent now. 'Since she was a tiny *bambina,* signor. Why do you ask?'

Michael hesitated, tried to pick his words with care. 'When you recommended her to us yesterday you mentioned she wasn't happy. And when she came to us in the afternoon I could see she seemed afraid of being seen talking to us... To cut the story short something happened last night to make me certain she is being watched...'

Pietro was watching him with intent interest. 'Last night, signor?'

Michael nodded. 'Yes; I met her by accident on the waterfront.' He went on to explain what had happened, finishing: 'It upset her so much she wanted me to find another guide. When I argued with her she finally gave in, saying: "It is only for two days and surely that could cause no trouble"... I've been puzzling ever since what she meant, and it suddenly occurred to me you might know.'

His story had made Pietro's teeth grind hard against the stem of his pipe. The old man sat silent for a long moment, examining the ruggedness of Michael's face and the compactness of his build. He liked what he saw and a sudden excited gleam came into his shrewd eyes.

'So you would like to know why my little *piccinina* is unhappy, signor. Very well, I will tell you. But to understand you must first understand this island, signor. Here it is like a dictatorship. All the wealth has got into the hands of a few, and the wealthiest of those is a young cockerel called Sabastian Cerone.'

Michael started. 'Cerone. We've already met him. He introduced himself yesterday evening.'

Pietro spat his dislike on the carpet of the lounge. 'A mongrel, signor. And yet his father was a fine man. I know – I used to work in his fishing fleet in those days.' Pietro put his skinny elbows on the table, leaned forward. 'The thing started years ago, signor, when Sabastian and Tina were children. The boy was different in those days – perhaps because his father was alive to use the stick – and he and Tina played together from the days they were infants until she went abroad to school. Sabastian was like an elder brother to her, and to give the mongrel his due I believe he thought the world of her. Whenever she came home on holiday he would be the first on the jetty to meet her, and when she finally came home to stay he threw one of the biggest parties the island has ever seen.

'This would be four years ago?'

Pietro rubbed his chin, nodded. 'About that, signor. And if the young mongrel had played his cards right he'd probably be married to her by this time because she was fond of him and lonely after her mother died. But for a mercy he was already taking too much for granted – he'd forgotten that both of them had changed in six years and that he couldn't own her just because they had been friends as children. It saved the *piccinina,* thank the Saints, because soon afterwards his father did him the one cruel trick of his life – he died and left Sabastian all his money. That opened up the flaw in his nature and we all saw the kind of man he was.'

The old fisherman jabbed his pipe fiercely at Michael. 'Money and power, signor – they ruin a man far quicker than wine. We soon began hearing stories – how a man here had been discharged because he was too old, another because he was too sickly. Then there was the food crisis – he had an agent corner it to lift the prices ... some of the peasants nearly starved that winter. Tina wouldn't believe it at first – she actually used to defend him and to quarrel with those who attacked him…'

She would be loyal like that, Michael thought. She had that quality which made a man feel he had missed something very precious in life. He listened intently to the old fisherman.

'He was very sure of himself now, signor, in his silk shirts, linen suits, and his sports car. The whole island belonged to him and nobody dared refuse him anything. So two years ago when he got drunk at a stag party of his business associates and boasted of his engagement to Tina, it did not matter that he had not yet asked her. He could repair that little omission the next day…'

The old man's face was a huge, wicked grin. 'He went round the next day, signor – very formal in a fine suit – to propose marriage. Maria, Tina's stepmother, was delighted – she loves money as much as the Devil loves a bad priest – but by this time Tina had found out the truth and refused him. He argued, pleaded and quarrelled with her, but she wouldn't budge an inch and so finally he had to swallow his pride and go.'

'Good for her,' Michael commented.

Pietro's expression changed, became fierce. 'Good for her, as you say, signor – she will be the lackey of no man, however rich, and I love her for it. But you must understand the situation now. Like all men of power and money Sabastian can neither bear nor afford to be laughed at – and the whole island was laughing when they found out. So to puff up his vanity the fool made a boast – more of a vow than a boast according to those who heard it – that he would marry her if it was the last thing that he did. And if anyone got in his way they had better take care.'

Pietro spat his disgust on the carpet again. 'And so the filthy business started. Little things at first, such as pestering her when she left school or when she went shopping. When that didn't frighten her his men began working on her friends. There was one, Emilio – a gentle lad she had known for years. They were nothing but friends but the poor child had no one else to go out with. One night he was beaten up by two fishermen and made to leave the island. Another youngster, Vittorio, was beaten up for taking her to a cinema. After that, for their sakes, she would not go out with anyone – not that there were any lads left with the guts to ask her. The girls too were afraid, and so today the child has hardly a friend of her own generation.'

Michael's expression was incredulous. 'It seems impossible in the twentieth century. Couldn't she make a complaint – go to the police for protection?'

Pietro shrugged. 'He isn't a fool, signor. He is never involved himself – he pays his men well to keep quiet.'

'Then why does she stay here? Why

doesn't she go to the mainland and get away from him?'

'I tell her that myself, signor, but it is easy for us to talk. As I say, Sabastian is no fool and has set the trap tight. Carlo, her father, used to be the ship-chandler for the fishing fleet that now belongs to Sabastian. What is easier for him than to give that trade elsewhere, with the understanding it would all come back if she married him.'

'And he has done that?'

'The mongrel has done more than that, signor. He has tried to intimidate people who still deal with old Carlo. Things are so bad with him now that only Tina's salary keeps them going. That is why her step-mother, may the Saints punish her, is always nagging at her to give way.'

'She has a brother, hasn't she? Doesn't he help at all?'

Pietro gave a growl of disgust. 'The young fool costs them more than the wages he gives them. A cousin of Sabastian, Guido Barti, pretends to be his friend and is always getting him into trouble. Anything, you see, signor, to make them poorer and so force her hand.' Hate gleamed like fire in the old fisherman's fierce eyes. *'Per Bacco,* how I hate that mongrel. The times I have wished myself twenty years younger...'

Michael was frowning. 'So that would be why she looked so anxious last night. She was thinking of me.'

Pietro eyed him through a cloud of acrid smoke. 'That would be the reason, signor. She never knows what the jealous mongrel will do next. But of course,' he added slyly, watching the young man's troubled face, 'she knew in her heart you were quite safe, leaving as you do tomorrow.'

Michael nodded slowly. At that moment Wilkinson entered the lounge, carrying a cup of coffee.

'Hello there! Is everything fixed up?'

With an effort Michael flung off his mood and turned to him. 'Yes. Pietro here has got us a car. I'm to fetch it in twenty minutes.'

The old fisherman rose, nodded at Wilkinson and hitched his jeans around his lean hips. 'And I must get down to my boat now. *Buon giorno, signori,* and have a good day.'

The early morning sun dug greedy golden fingers in Cristina's hair as she stood waiting for Pietro. His leathery face wore a grin of pleasure and there was a curious jauntiness in his steps as he approached her, his heavy seaboots clumping on the jetty.

'Hello, *piccinina.* What can I do for you this morning?'

'I've come to see about the car. Have you managed to borrow one?'

'I have just come from the hotel, *piccinina,* and everything is arranged. The young

Englishman is going to fetch the car, and when you go round to the hotel it will be waiting for you.'

Under his bushy brows his keen eyes watched her as she thanked him. He scowled and motioned her to come nearer to him. '*Piccinina*. When I called to see you yesterday, something was wrong. The shadow of it was on your face. The same shadow is there today. What have they done to you this time?'

She looked quickly away and did not answer.

'Tell me *piccinina*. You cannot hide things from old Pietro.'

The gay brightness of her yellow frock was a sharp contrast to her expression as she turned back to him. 'If I tell you, you must promise me you will do nothing. I don't want you getting into more trouble over me.'

Pietro's leathery old face was fierce. 'I make no promises, *piccinina*. But now you must tell me or I shall find out in other ways.' One of the jetty benches stood near them and he motioned her to it. 'Sit down, *piccinina,* and tell me what has happened.'

Cristina walked over to the bench and sat disconsolately down. 'It's Giuseppe. Guido has got him into trouble again and this time it could be very serious.'

Pietro pulled his pipe from the pocket of his jeans, peered into the bowl, and put a match to the half-burned contents. He then

59

sat alongside the girl, his rough voice curiously gentle.

'Tell me what the boy has done this time *piccinina*.'

She told him about Giuseppe's escapade in the piazza two evenings ago and the resultant damage to old Carmillo's bicycle. Pietro's blue eyes stared at her fiercely.

'You say it was Guido who dared him to do this?'

She nodded. 'Yes; and I'm certain I know why. I met Sabastian yesterday; he was waiting for me when I left school. From what he said I realise he must have been behind it.'

Pietro muttered a fierce sea-oath under his breath. 'That cockerel again… *Santa Maria,* is there no one here man enough to stand up to him?'

She tried to take the sting out of his anger. 'I slapped his face yesterday. You should have seen his expression.'

Pietro stared at her. 'In the street!'

She nodded, explaining what had happened. Pietro's enormous guffaw of delight sent a cluster of pigeons flying for safety. '*Santissima Madonna,* that is wonderful, *piccinina.* Wonderful! You've more spirit than all the young men of this island put together.' He spat his disgust to the jetty. 'In my day a cockerel like that would not have lasted five minutes. But today it is only money that counts – they crawl on their bellies and let

themselves be trodden into the ground for it.'
Then his expression changed. 'But this is not
helping you, *piccinina*. Let me see how much
I have got.'

He fumbled in the rear pocket of his jeans,
pulled out a thin wad of paper money. Licking a thumb he counted it and gave a grimace
of disgust. 'Only fourteen hundred – it is
nothing, I know. But you are welcome to it…'

Her hand was on his wrist. 'No; it isn't
necessary. I have this work you found me –
that is why I accepted it.'

He pushed the money at her. 'You'll still
be short. Take it, *piccinina*.'

'Not all of it, then. What will you do for
food?'

His great laugh boomed out again. 'Don't
worry about that. Old Pietro can always find
something for his belly.' He rubbed his
whiskery chin with regret. 'I only wish it
were more. No one on the island is more
deserving of help.'

'You are certain you can spare it?'

He scowled at her fiercely. '*Santa Maria;*
the fuss you make over a few lire. Take it,
woman, and stop nagging me.'

She laughed at him. 'All right, it's pay day
next Friday at the school – I can give it back
to you then.'

He scowled again, threw out a brown arm
and pointed to the sea. 'I don't want paying
back next Friday. I want you to take the ship

to the mainland. Go north – to Genoa or Milan – there's supposed to be plenty of work up there. Get away from Sabastian and this prison.'

'Don't start all that over again, please. You know perfectly well I can't go.'

Pietro spat his disgust down to the jetty again. 'Of course – your father and brother. *Santissima Madonna;* for how much longer must this waste go on?'

She sat motionless, staring blindly across the bay at the high, green cliffs. Pietro leaned towards her, his voice gentle again. '*Piccinina,* listen to me for a moment. I am old and I know more about men than you. They are like earthenware jars – once they are broken they cannot be mended again. No matter how you fit the pieces, there will always be a leak somewhere...'

She turned on him resentfully. 'You're talking about my father, aren't you?'

His old fierce eyes did not fall away. 'Yes, *piccinina,* I am. Once he was a fine, determined man, but when your mother died something in him died too. He will never be the same man again, and it is wrong that a young girl like you should waste her life on him. It is wrong and it is dangerous. Because what I said about men applies to women too.'

'You think that one day I will break ... like an earthenware jar?'

'It could happen, *piccinina.* And it must

not... *Per Bacco;* it must not. That is why I say take the ship and go. Go while there is still time.'

'And Giuseppe. What about him?'

'Giuseppe will never grow into a man while he has your skirts to hide behind. It is bad for him.'

'I suppose you realise that without the money I earn they would be homeless in a month.'

'Men have been homeless before, *piccinina*. There is still the sun and the sea and the Good God above.'

Her face was set. 'It's no use, Pietro. I'm not going. Don't talk about it any more, please...' At that moment, over his shoulder, she noticed half a dozen men coming in their direction, making for a cluster of fishing boats that nosed against the harbour side of the jetty. A huge, barrel-chested young man with a mop of black hair and a swarthy, rugged face led the party. He was wearing a pair of blue serge trousers and a chequered American-type shirt thrown ostentatiously open to display a black fuzz of chest hair. Alongside him was the man who had followed Cristina the previous night, small and thin with a shifty, ferret-like face.

'Guido, Mario and a crowd of Sabastian's men,' she told Pietro tightly as he noticed her gaze and half-turned to follow it. 'Coming to service the boats, I suppose.'

As the men drew level with them the big man at their head grinned and nodded. '*Giorno,* Tina. *Giorno,* old man.'

Her contemptuous glance passed right through him. He grinned awkwardly, threw a glance at Mario alongside him, then turned back to her. 'Give Peppi a message for me, will you, Tina? Tell him we'll all be in Santi's bar this afternoon.'

Her voice was vibrant with anger. 'He'll get no message from me, Guido.'

He pretended to look surprised. 'Why not? What's wrong with you this morning?'

Her lips curled. 'You can't guess, of course.'

There was little subtlety in Guido and even less imagination.

'I suppose you're blaming me for what happened on Thursday night.'

'Aren't you to blame?' she asked bitterly. 'You and Sabastian.'

Guido's second attempt to look surprised would not have had Sabastian's approval. 'Sabastian! He'd nothing to do with it. It was a little bet, that's all. For fun. I didn't know Peppi couldn't drive.'

She knew it would have been wiser to have left the matter there for the moment. But Guido's crudely-concealed mockery and the grinning faces of the men around him were too much for her.

'You're a liar. Sabastian put you up to it. And anyway, it's not the first time you've got him into trouble. Leave him alone in the future. He's only a boy.'

Her stinging attack left him uncertain. At first he tried to bluster, gave a laugh, but as he noticed the grins of the other men were now directed at him his swarthy face darkened.

'Don't talk like a fool, Cristina. You can't blame me every time the kid drinks too much and gets himself into trouble. I'm not his father.'

It was all Pietro had been waiting for. His sudden bark was like the backfire of a primed engine. 'Careful what you say, mongrel. The girl's right – everyone knows how you dance to Sabastian's tune.'

To Guido, playing a role beyond his talents, the interruption came as a relief. He turned with a swagger on the old fisherman. 'So – the old dog with the big bark! Be careful, old dog, that one day a man does not pick you up and rattle your bones.'

Pietro's lips came back ferociously. 'And what man would that be, mongrel? I didn't know there were any men left on this island.'

Guido put his muscular hands on his hips, sneered at him. 'An old dog without teeth. Hiding behind his years. Stop yapping, old man.'

Pietro's stringy hand leapt back, clutched the rear pocket of his jeans. His growl was as deep as that of an old bear. 'No teeth, mongrel? Are you sure? Would you like to snap again and find out?'

There was a sudden hush on the jetty. Then Cristina ran forward and caught the old man's arm. Her voice was sharp, anxious. 'Stop it, Pietro. Stop being ridiculous.'

Pietro's hand did not move, nor did his fierce eyes leave Guido's face. 'Leave her alone, mongrel. Leave her – do you hear?'

Cristina tugged at him. 'Stop it. Stop talking like that. Come away.'

He allowed her to pull him back to the seat. Guido gave a mocking laugh. 'That's better. Hide behind her skirt. You're wise, old man.'

Cristina swung round on him. 'Have you gone crazy too? Leave us alone before there's more trouble.'

He shrugged his heavy shoulders. 'I didn't ask the old fool to quarrel with me.'

She turned her back on him. He watched them sullenly for a moment, then motioned abruptly for the men to follow him. They went down a flight of steps on the inside of the jetty and vanished into the boats moored there. Cristina turned to Pietro. Fear for his safety had not yet left her and it made her voice severe.

'Aren't things bad enough already without your behaving like this? You must be losing your mind, to start threatening them with a knife.'

The old man scowled and jammed himself sullenly against the back of the seat. Arms grimly folded, pipe hanging from his clenched teeth like a tusk, he resembled a fierce old walrus as he glowered without speaking across the bay. Cristina's voice trembled on the brink between reproach and affection.

'It won't do me any good, your behaving like that. And it might get you into very serious trouble.'

The old fisherman's growl was like the rumble of distant thunder. 'Let me tell you something, *piccinina*. If I were thirty years younger – no, twenty would be more than enough – I would be down among those boats at this moment, picking up that black-haired mongrel by his ears and dropping him into the sea. And then I would do something much better; I would go and find his cousin Sabastian. And I would take a knotted stick with me, as we used to do in the old days. We would go somewhere quiet and we would fight. But I would not stop when I had knocked him down – not I, Pietro. I would hit him until his ribs were smashed and his head broken and the blood running out of his mouth. Then, *piccinina*, he would never bother you again. Never...' For a moment Pietro's wrinkled eyelids closed tightly. 'Ah, how easy it is when one is young... *Santissima Madonna;* will you not make me young just for one day? Even one hour will be enough…'

'You mustn't talk like that. You mustn't be so blood-thirsty.' Then, as emotion burned her eyes like acid, she dropped her face against his shoulder, nuzzled it into the coarse blue cloth. 'But, oh, I do wish you were young again, Pietro. I wish that so very much…'

Yearning in the old man was like a great, sobbing thirst. Then his fierce eyes opened again and blazed wickedly at her, burning up the hint of moisture that dulled them. 'But I must warn you, *piccinina,* that you would not be safe with me. No girl was safe. I was a man – not one of these beaten dogs that drop their tails every time their master shouts at them.'

She laughed her affection for him with the tears running down her cheeks. 'I'd throw a bucket of water over you. I'd make you behave.'

He pulled a large coloured handkerchief from his pocket and dabbed at her cheeks. His voice was amazingly gentle now. 'You would not be safe whatever you threw over me, *piccinina.* But then I would not be safe either. I should find myself proposing marriage to you – something I have avoided like the plague all my life. So perhaps it is as well I am an old man.'

She caught hold of his hand, pressed it to

her cheek. 'You're not old. You'll never be old to me.' Her wet eyes were suddenly puzzled. 'Why is that – why have you never become tired and defeated like so many other old people on the island? You've been poor all your life, haven't you?'

Pietro's laugh boomed out triumphantly. 'Why, *piccinina?* Because I have never put my belly before my self-respect, that is why. Most men,' and his voice was infinitely contemptuous, 'they are like the pigeons in the piazza – they will fawn and coo and do anything to get their food. But not the eagle and not even the old crow. Perhaps they don't eat so well, *piccinina,* but they stay free.'

'They stay free,' she repeated slowly. 'Yes, of course.'

His gnarled hand pressed her smooth one tightly. 'That is why old Pietro has always loved you. The rest of the young women here – pah, they would sell their bodies and their souls to Sabastian for his money. But not you, *piccinina* … oh, I have loved you for that. But now I fear for you too. You have a weakness and Sabastian has found it – you love your father and brother too well. That is why I beg of you to leave the island before it is too late.'

She immediately pulled away, looked down at the small watch on her wrist. 'I shall have to go in a few minutes. I promised to be at the hotel at ten.'

Pietro scowled but for the moment dropped his entreaty. 'You're going out to the Grotto first, aren't you?'

She nodded. 'Mr Wilkinson is hoping it may be an attraction for tourists. At least so Mr Forbes said last night.'

Pietro's sharp ears pricked at her mention of Michael. 'The young Englishman told me he had seen you last night. What do you think of him?'

Colour tinted the girl's cheeks. 'He seems very nice. Why do you ask?'

Pietro did not miss her confusion and was more than satisfied. His voice was innocence itself when he answered. 'Nothing, *piccinina*. It is just that I like him myself. He has a good strong face and broad shoulders. He does not strut and yap like some of our puppies here, but when he bites he will bite hard and not let go.'

His tone and words disarmed her. 'Yes; I like him too. He seems very kind.' She rose quickly to her feet. 'I must go now. Thank you for everything, and keep out of trouble with Guido. Do you hear me?'

He grinned up at her. 'I hear, little mother. Don't worry about me.' The hopeful gleam had returned to his eyes as he called after her. 'Come and see me when you get back – I want to know how things have gone.'

CHAPTER 5

Wilkinson paused to mop his forehead. 'How much further is it?' he grunted.

Cristina pointed to the rising ground ahead of them. 'When we reach the top there we should be able to see it.'

The two Englishmen and the girl were making their way along the cliffs at the south side of the bay. The sun was fierce, burning through their clothes and giving the air a radiant quality, as though it were impregnated with golden dust. On their left high green hills rolled down to a series of headlands, the cliffs in turn dropping down to the lazily-moving turquoise sea. The scent of sage and wild thyme rose from the bushes alongside the path. Across the bay behind them the tiny bleached houses of Veronia gleamed like white teeth in the brilliant sunshine.

Cristina led the way up the narrow winding path, with Michael close behind her and Wilkinson trailing some distance behind. Watching the rise and fall of her bright hair made Michael think of the sea below. At the crest of the ridge she paused and pointed down. 'There it is. At the bottom of the cliff.'

Before them stood a sheer, three-hundred-foot headland. Unlike the others it was of bare rock, thrusting out like a great cruel face into the sea. At its base where rocks and sea met was a shadowy entrance.

Wilkinson came panting up alongside them. 'Where is it?' he muttered. When Cristina pointed it out to him he lifted a pair of binoculars and stared at it closely. His voice was disappointed as he handed the glasses to Michael. 'Doesn't look much from here. Just another cave as far as I can see.'

Michael saw he was right. All he could see through the binoculars was a dark entrance, perhaps fourteen feet high, with a wide cleft through which the sea appeared to enter. Terraced rocks, at the moment splashed by waves, ran round the foot of the headland. He turned to Cristina.

'Is there any way of getting into it except by boat?'

'Yes; there's a way down the other side of the headland.' She glanced doubtfully at the heavily-built Wilkinson. 'But it's rather a difficult climb.'

'Do people go into it?'

'No. As I told you last night it is believed to be haunted as well as dangerous.'

He smiled at her. 'And yet you seem to know a good deal about it. Have you ever been inside?'

She hesitated a moment. 'Yes. A long time ago when I was a child. A friend of mine took me – once by boat and the other time we climbed down the cliff. My father was very angry when he found out – he thinks it's much too dangerous to enter or even approach.'

Wilkinson frowned. 'Why is it so dangerous? It doesn't look it from here.'

She pointed down to the sea around the entrance. Michael noticed now that it was a different colour, a cold green against the blue of the surrounding water. 'The fishermen say that sometimes when there are clouds over the island a sobbing noise comes from it and the sea around becomes terribly rough. Only three years ago a boy fishing for lobsters was sucked under and drowned. And right through the centuries there are tales of boats being lost. The fishermen say this often happens when there is no wind and the rest of the sea is calm.'

'Funny business,' Wilkinson grunted, taking the binoculars again. 'I suppose this sobbing noise is the reason it's supposed to be haunted?'

'Yes; it's part of the superstition.' Somewhat shyly Cristina repeated the legend to Wilkinson. 'The clouds over the island are supposed to represent Tiberius's anger, the sobbing sound comes from the lovers as they're being dragged off the rocks, and the churning of the sea comes from their death struggles.'

Wilkinson grimaced. 'It's a meaty enough

story, anyway. You say you've been inside. What's it like?'

'It's very eerie – at least I thought so. Shadowy, very cold, with a peculiar smell of damp earth… But there isn't much to see. It's quite large – it opens out once one is through the entrance.'

'Any stalagmites or anything like that?'

'No; I don't remember seeing any.'

Wilkinson's look of disappointment was returning. 'If there's nothing unusual inside I don't see how we can use it as a gimmick.' He glanced again at Cristina. 'This sobbing noise and the churning of the sea – do you believe they really happen?'

She hesitated. 'I don't know what to believe. There are so many reports it's difficult to believe it can all be superstition.'

'If this sobbing noise is loud, couldn't it be heard in Veronia? Or at least in some of the nearer villages.'

'No. They say the formation of the cliffs prevents the sound carrying very far. And there are no villages around here.'

'How often is it supposed to happen? Once a day? Once a week?'

'Oh, no – nothing as often as that. It's hard to say – people tend to stay away from these cliffs and fishermen won't come near the headland. But people don't claim it happens often – certainly no more than a few times a year.'

Wilkinson gave a grunt of disappointment as he turned to Michael. 'I thought it was queer that no other agency had got in first... It might draw a few cranks – an odd couple with a suicide pact – but the mass of tourists want more than a big empty cave to stare into. The Med.'s full of 'em already. Pity, but there it is.'

Michael knew he was right but felt reluctant to leave the matter there. 'Don't you think we ought to take a look in it before making up our minds? Perhaps we could hire a boat this afternoon and take a trip out.'

The heat and exertion had made Wilkinson testy. 'What – with all the fishermen on the island scared to come near the place? And I'm not climbing down that cliff – not to look into an empty cave. There's no point in it when Miss Delfano has seen inside it herself. Let's cut our losses, Mike, and get back to the hotel. I'm dying for a drink.'

They followed him silently back along the narrow cliff path. He kept ahead of them until the next hill and then fell behind again, his white shirt dark with sweat. They slowed their pace, and on the crest of the last hill waited for him to join them. The great arc of the bay shimmered like a burnished blue mirror. A dusty brown road stretched out below them, looping out from behind a hill to the cliff edge and then swinging back inland again. An old Fiat stood on the loop of the road and Wilkinson gave a grunt of relief as he reached the hill crest and saw it.

'Not before time. Another half a mile of this and I'd have given up and died.'

They reached the Fiat three minutes later. Its shabby interior smelt strongly of vegetables. On her insistence Cristina sat at the back behind Michael, Wilkinson alongside him. The clutch slipped badly and the Fiat juddered as Michael backed it round.

The road to Veronia took them inland, behind a steep hill. Brown dust rose behind them in clouds. But the air on their faces was cool and Wilkinson took deep breaths of it. 'This is better. Mother McCree, how my feet ache!'

They passed a donkey cart loaded with onions. Peasants, scratching at the thin soil of the hills, turned to stare at them. Cristina leaned over Michael's shoulder and pointed the way. 'Turn left at the fork. Then straight on over the bridge.'

The exhilaration he had felt on her arrival that morning was accentuated by her nearness and gave an added novelty to everything he saw. They passed a tiny cottage, a grove of olive trees, a hillside of vines. They rattled over a bridge that crossed a dried-up stream and passed a bank gay with ripening tomatoes. He waved a hand to a crowd of peasants walking up the road and grinned at the antics of a small boy trying to climb on the back of a donkey. He felt immensely alive.

They entered Veronia, shuddering over cobblestones that made the Fiat's springs grumble their protest. The streets were narrow and crowded with children. Cristina leaned forward again, her arm touching his shoulder. 'To the left now... Then first right and keep going straight on until you reach the piazza.'

They turned on to the waterfront where he had met her the previous night. A boat was loading watermelons from a lorry. Another three hundred yards and they entered the piazza. Steam rose from the Fiat's radiator like hot breath as Michael pulled up outside the hotel. His regret that the morning expedition was over was tempered by the knowledge that the afternoon still lay ahead. Then he heard Wilkinson.

'I don't think we want to see any more, do you?'

Michael turned to face him. 'What did you say?'

'I said I don't think we want to see any more. The Grotto was the one thing that might have been an attraction, but without that it's just another small island. I don't see any point in spending more money looking round it.'

From the corner of his eye Michael saw Cristina involuntary draw back. It was a diffident movement that made him hotly resentful of Wilkinson.

'Surely there must be plenty of other places to see. We haven't been round a quarter of the island yet.'

Wilkinson shook his head. 'There's nothing else, Mike. Without the Grotto it's just another island – I can think of dozens like it and better. We need something more to attract tourists.'

Michael could see the girl's embarrassment and felt a desire to hurt Wilkinson. 'Why don't you be honest and say it's because your feet hurt? We've got a whole day here yet – we can't just sit around drinking beer.'

Wilkinson stared at him in surprise. 'What's biting you all of a sudden? I'm only trying to save your father money. I tell you this island is no good for tourists. And so the best thing we can do is cut our losses until the boat arrives tomorrow afternoon.'

'I'm not sitting here until the boat comes. I want to see more than this.' Michael swung round on the embarrassed girl. 'Will you please come this afternoon, as arranged? I'd like to see the centre of the island and one of the villages.'

Cristina's voice was low and unsure. 'But if your friend does not want to go…'

'If my friend doesn't want to go he's free to say in the hotel,' Michael said curtly. He attempted a smile to reassure her. 'It's all right. Please come.'

She threw an uncertain glance at Wilkinson. 'Very well; if you're quite sure it's all right. What about the car? We can't use it in the centre of the island.'

'I'll return it now,' he said, helping her out.

She hesitated, as though already regretting her decision. Then, with a quick, anxious shake of her head, she hurried down the piazza towards the shop.

Michael, already regretting his quick temper, turned to Wilkinson who, red-faced and sulky, was climbing out of the car. 'Sorry if I was a bit short, Jack. But I want to see a bit more of the place before we leave.'

The tiny devil of malice in Wilkinson would not allow him to forgive quite so quickly. 'See the place if you want to – that's your business. But do you need the girl – at five hundred lire an hour? You seem to forget I'm responsible to your father for the expenses of this trip.'

The brusqueness returned to Michael's voice. 'If that's what's worrying you, I'll pay her out of my own pocket. Satisfied now?'

The remark that quivered on the tip of Wilkinson's tongue would have sparked off a first-class quarrel. With an effort he swallowed it back and tramped morosely up the steps of the hotel.

CHAPTER 6

The afternoon sun was intense, a weariness in the limbs. At the top of the bush-covered hill Cristina turned, called back to Michael. 'There's a path here – it runs straight down to Proccio. It isn't far – no more than half a mile.'

She was standing in an attitude of unconscious grace, one leg braced against the slope of the hillside. The striped cotton shirt and faded jeans she was wearing betrayed the shapeliness of her figure. Michael grinned ruefully up at her. 'A bit of shade won't come amiss. Nor will a cool drink.' He pushed his way through the dry scented bushes and came up alongside her. A faint breeze cleared the ridge and cooled his sweat-soaked body. The sea lay below them again, stretching out to an infinite, rust-hazed horizon. In a valley in the cliffs a small village lay in the sun.

Goats were grazing on the hillside. The goatherd, half-asleep on a pony, lifted his head and stared at them as they passed by. He was a tall thin man, wearing a broad-brimmed straw hat and a jerkin over a faded yellow shirt. His trousers were of goat-skin and he wore long, sharp spurs. His eyes followed them as they approached the village.

A dirt road ran round the base of the hill. It led them through a grove of fig trees, and the shade was like a cool breeze on their faces. A few houses lined the road, their drawn shutters like closed eyelids. Massed flowers burned in the sun and the air was heavy with the scent of heliotrope and datura.

The cool, cobbled streets of the village closed round them, leading them down to the sea. They passed a high wall, matted and aflame with bougainvillaea. Fat, sun-flecked pigeons, stupid in the heat, barely found the strength to waddle out of their way. An old woman in a black dress sat on the steps of her house, nodding over her sewing. Ahead they could hear the cool, running murmur of the sea.

They passed through a narrow street that was all shadow and sunlight. High on a wall two linnets chattered at them from a yellow cage. A huge string of onions hung from a hook alongside a door. Then they came out on a narrow waterfront and the glare of sun and sea dazzled their eyes. Cristina pointed to a small shop under a tall, angular house.

'I'm afraid they won't sell beer. But the wine will be cool.'

Two tables stood outside the shop, receiving shade from a small canvas awning. A bead curtain hung over the doorway and a bell tinkled as Michael held it aside for Cristina to enter. He followed her into a small rectangular room of roughly plastered walls and a floor of scrubbed brick. A few empty tables were scattered about, served by plain wooden benches. A counter stood across the far end of the room and behind it casks of wine lay in a huge rack. A door draped by another bead curtain stood alongside the counter.

As they waited, an old woman in a black smock that fitted her like bark shuffled through it. Michael saw her eyes become instantly wary as they fell on Cristina. She darted a swift glance at him, muttered something he could not understand and shuffled back through the bead curtain. A few moments later a man who might have been her son appeared, tying an apron around himself. He was grossly fat and from his appearance had been asleep. There was a guarded note in his voice as he greeted them. Cristina asked him for wine and then turned to Michael. 'Do you wish to stay in here or go outside?'

'I think I'd like it outside. It should be quite cool under the awning.'

She made no protest and they took one of the pavement tables. In the tiny harbour in front of them a line of fishing boats nodded like tired sheep. The shopkeeper brought them a beaker and two glasses.'

'*Grazie, signorina. Grazie, signore.*'

He retreated behind the bead curtain and watched them a moment before waddling away. Michael poured out the wine. It was local, slightly rough but very cool. He leaned back in his chair with a sigh of pleasure and smiled at her.

'I hope you're not tired. I've given you a hard afternoon.'

She shook her head quickly. 'No; I've enjoyed it. It has been a change for me.'

Her words brought him an odd satisfying gladness. At that moment the bead curtain parted and the old woman appeared. Without glancing at them she shuffled hurriedly away, her slippers flopping on the cobbles. She was making for an alley thirty yards away, and she threw a glance back at them that was oddly furtive before disappearing into it.

Her conduct reminded Michael of all he had heard that morning from Pietro. Cristina had turned slightly to watch the old woman. Now, as she faced the table again and stared down at the glass in her hand, he leaned forward.

'What's the matter, Cristina? Are you afraid she's going to let Sabastian know about this?'

The glass in her hand jerked, spilling wine on the table. Her wide, frightened eyes lifted to him. 'You know...? But how? Who told you?'

'Pietro. This morning.'

She shook her head in acute distress. 'It was wrong of him. He had no right to say anything.'

'It was my fault. Last night I guessed something was wrong and I couldn't help asking him. Is it all true? Does he have you watched wherever you go?'

'Please … I don't want to talk about it. It has been such a happy day – don't let us spoil it.'

His rough-hewn face was dogged. 'I haven't the time to wait – I leave tomorrow. I want to know if there is anything I can do to help before I go. If there is, please tell me.'

'There is nothing you can do – nothing anyone can do. Please drink your wine and say no more about it.'

'But I want to know if all the things Pietro said are true. Has he really made you friend-less? Has he ruined your father's business? And is he influencing your brother and getting him into trouble? I want to know, Cristina.'

His sympathy was like a lancet, pressing harder on the aching cyst inside her. Her eyes suddenly ached unbearably and panic-stricken she closed them, fighting to hold back her tears. His anger spilled over.

'I wouldn't have believed such a thing possible these days. The man must be crazy. Haven't you any friends who have the guts to stand up to him?'

He knew the answer before asking the question and went on savagely: 'Who was the rat-faced creature following you last night?'

Her voice was dull, hopeless. 'That was Mario. Sabastian often uses him to follow me.'

'Is he the one who gets your brother into trouble – Sabastian's cousin?'

'No. That is Guido, a bigger, younger man. You may not have seen him yet.'

He jerked his head at the wineshop. 'What about this old woman? Will she be employed by him?'

'I shouldn't think so. But people are so strange... They don't like Sabastian and what he is doing, and yet because he pays them well for information they still help him.'

The loneliness in her voice made him wince with pity. 'You mean that because this old woman knows she'll get paid for the tip she's putting a phone call through telling him you're out here with me?'

'I could be wrong. Please don't say any-thing to her when she comes back. It wouldn't do any good, and this time it does not matter because he already knows what I am doing today.'

He lit a cigarette in an effort to control his anger. He found himself repeating the same arguments he had used on Pietro.

'Hasn't your father ever tried to do

anything about this? Haven't you ever made a protest to the police?'

He could not decide at which question her faintly bitter smile was directed. 'What could I prove to the police? He is far too clever for that.'

'Then why don't you leave the island? You're an intelligent, attractive girl and you speak English perfectly. Surely you could get a job on the mainland. If you couldn't you could go to England. There's plenty of work there.'

There might have been bars across the bright blue sky from the expression in her eyes. He remembered the dependence of her family on her salary and shook his head resentfully. 'Surely your brother ought to help more. How old is he?'

'Eighteen.'

'And you say Sabastian uses this cousin of his to get your brother into trouble. Is Giuseppe in any trouble at the moment?'

He saw her flinch and knew he had guessed right. 'He is, isn't he? What kind of trouble?'

Her loyalty to her family was strong and at first she would not answer. But he was as obstinate and determined as she, and eventually he prised from her the story of Giuseppe's escapade in the lorry. When she had finished his face was dark with anger.

'I see – anything to put you in his debt or

make things more difficult for your father. The man must be a devil.'

She made an uncertain, troubled gesture of her hands. 'He wasn't always like this... Once he was like an elder brother to me – that's what makes things so much worse. He was the friend I told you about who took me to the Grotto. The change seemed to come when his father died. And, of course, our quarrel started when I refused to marry him. He could never bear to be laughed at, and it was much worse now that he was the most important man on the island. I think he was afraid it would undermine his influence... He swore he would marry me and now it seems to have become an obsession with him. At first I was his only target, but now he attacks innocent people too. Sometimes I'm afraid to think where it will all end...'

Her voice broke off abruptly and Michael heard the flop-flop of slippers on the cobblestones. He started to rise as he saw the old woman approaching but Cristina caught his arm. 'Please... I asked you to say nothing. It can only cause trouble for me.'

He dropped reluctantly back into his chair. The old woman, who had noticed his expression, threw him a baleful glance as she disappeared behind the bead curtain. Cristina met his eyes.

'I think we ought to be going now. Please finish your wine.'

They passed through the narrow streets of the village and came out on the dirt road. On the hillside above the goatherd watched them turn along it in the direction of Veronia.

Five minutes of silence passed between them and then Michael turned to her. 'I want you to do me a favour. Let me give you the balance of the money you need for the bicycle.'

Her eyes were wide, a little frightened. 'Give it to me? But why should you do that?'

His craggy eyebrows drew together at the question. 'Because I want to help you, I suppose. Will you take it?'

She allowed herself no time for temptation. 'No. You've been very good to me already but I can't take money I haven't earned.'

He laid both hands gently on her shoulders and turned her towards him. 'If you must be so very English, then be my guide tonight. Take me to the best restaurant in Veronia and have dinner with me. Will you do that?'

For a moment she smiled back. 'That is the same as giving me the money.'

'Please come. I want it very much.'

'No, Michael. If I went with you I should not take the money. But it is impossible … we would be watched. I'm watched everywhere I go. Can't you understand that?'

'What if you are watched? What can Sabastian do to me?' Her nearness was making him feel as indestructible as a god.

'Let me see you tonight, Cristina. Please.'

His hands were still on her shoulders and suddenly tightened. The twin images of herself in his eyes grew nearer. Then she caught a glimpse of the hill behind him and instantly she was all fear and resistance, pulling fiercely away from him.

'No, Michael! It is too dangerous. Please don't come near me...'

He swung sharply round. High on the crest of the hill he could see the motionless figure of the goatherd on his pony.

Her frightened words were like a fugitive's stumbling feet. 'You see ... it is everywhere I go. Men and women ... sometimes even children... I can't go out with you, Michael... Please come now. We must get back to Veronia quickly.'

She ran along the road. He followed her, his face black and his eyes sullen with anger. He turned again and the goatherd was still there, a motionless figure against the clear blue sky.

CHAPTER 7

Wilkinson stepped out on the hotel verandah and turned in disgust to Michael. 'All
the tables are full. What do you want to do
– go down to the pavement?'

Michael shrugged. 'If we want a drink
outside I suppose we've no choice.'

They found an empty table on the right of
the verandah, and Wilkinson motioned a
young waiter towards them. 'Two beers. As
cold as you can find 'em. All right?'

'*Si, signor.*'

Wilkinson leaned back and gazed around
the piazza. 'Not as crowded as last night,
but they'll be back tomorrow – Sunday is
the festival night. Thank the lord we'll have
gone.'

Michael made no comment. His eyes were
on a table further down the pavement where
four men were sitting. Two were middle-
aged, linen-suited, prosperous in appearance. The third was a broad-shouldered,
black-haired man in his early twenties,
wearing a chequered shirt thrown open at
the neck. Although Michael did not know
him he was Guido, Sabastian's cousin. The
fourth man was Sabastian, a dandy in a

black, tight-waisted blouse with a yellow silk scarf at his throat. His keen black eyes had spotted Wilkinson and Michael the moment they left the hotel verandah and had followed them to their table.

Wilkinson gave a grunt of recognition. 'That's the young chap who came to see us yesterday, isn't it – the one who offered to build a new hotel if we recommended the island?'

Michael gave a tight nod. 'Cerone. Sabastian Cerone.'

The slim, athletic young Italian rose and approached them. He spoke to Wilkinson, ignoring Michael. *'Buona sera, signore.* Have you enjoyed your day on the island?'

'I suppose you've come to know what we think of it?' Wilkinson asked as he pushed out a chair.

Sabastian's expression was apologetic. 'My friends over there are very keen to know. Two of them are the business associates I mentioned to you yesterday.'

Wilkinson saw the three men were watching him and turned a trifle uncomfortably back to Sabastian. 'I don't like telling you this, signor, but frankly the island's no good for us. The Grotto was my main hope, but I've found out today it has no touristic possibilities. So I'm afraid I can't put in a favourable report.'

For a moment Sabastian's mobile face

91

betrayed his disappointment. Then he gave a laugh of incredulity. 'You are disappointed with the Grotto, signor? But surely it is unique. I've always believed that one day people would come from all over the world to see it. Didn't Miss Delfano tell you that the islanders believe it is haunted by two lovers and their murderers? That every so often a great sobbing sound comes from it and the sea around it becomes a maelstrom?'

Wilkinson shifted impatiently. 'Yes; she told us all that. But you can't expect people to come...'

'You don't believe these things happen?' Sabastian interrupted sharply. 'Is that it?' He leaned across the table, his sharp eyes on Wilkinson's face. 'If that is so I can put your doubts at rest, signor. For I have seen it happen with my own eyes.'

For a moment Wilkinson's interest stirred again. 'You have? How often does it happen?'

'Not often. No one knows exactly, but perhaps six times a year... But I know it does happen and so does everyone else on the island.'

'But that's the trouble – if it doesn't happen often it's no use. We can't bring people all the way here on the off-chance they'll be lucky. And there's nothing else of interest on the island. The only way the Grotto could be an attraction would be if a performance could be guaranteed weeks in advance. And that's obviously impossible.'

Sabastian's reply made both Wilkinson and Michael stare at him curiously. 'I could let you know a day or two beforehand, signor.'

'You could? How could you do that.'

Sabastian smiled, shrugged. 'I have a way. I have studied the Grotto with great interest.'

'Could you be certain?'

'Not absolutely certain. But near enough.'

'What's the longest notice you could give us?'

The Italian hesitated. 'A day for sure. Perhaps two, but not for certain.'

Wilkinson sat back with a grunt of disappointment. 'Then it's no use. We couldn't make the necessary arrangements in time, not even if we flew people here. And in any case half a dozen times a year isn't enough. It's a damned shame but there it is. Sorry.'

There was a brief, taut silence. Shadows from the street lamps, shifting across the young Italian's face, made his expression dark and sullen. His tone was subtly changed as he turned to Michael. 'What about you, signor? Perhaps you have found the island more attractive than your colleague?'

Michael made no attempt to hide his dislike. 'I did until this morning. Then I changed my mind.'

Sabastian's voice was as smooth as a steel blade being drawn from a velvet scabbard.

'And what was it that changed your mind, signor.'

'I don't like the way the big fish here try to gobble up the little ones. Is that clear enough or would you like it put another way?'

The shadows could not conceal the animosity on either of their faces. 'In that case, signor, if you do not find the island to your liking, it is perhaps a good thing you are leaving tomorrow.'

The barely-hidden threat brought up all the tough, north-country obstinacy in Michael. It thrust caution and compliance aside like two angry, muscular arms. 'Who said I was leaving tomorrow?'

The Italian's dark eyes narrowed. 'You told me yourself. Yesterday evening.'

'What if I did? I've changed my mind. Any objections?'

Wilkinson let out a startled grunt of protest. For a moment Sabastian's face was thunder black at the announcement. Then he gave a thin-lipped, pointed smile. 'If the island affects your health and temper so much, signor, they will only grow worse if you stay. My advice to your friend, who seems wiser than you, is to persuade you to change your mind and go.'

Their eyes measured one another like swords. Then Sabastian turned sharply and returned to his table. Michael watched him go, his fists hard rocks on the table. Wilkinson was staring at him open-mouthed. 'What's come over you? Have you gone crazy?'

Michael told him everything he had heard that day about Cristina. When he had finished sweat was glistening on Wilkinson's florid face. He dabbed at it with a handkerchief. 'For God's sake, Mike, you can't get mixed up in a thing like this. These islanders can be devils where women are concerned, and if you stay on here it'll be obvious what you're staying for. And anyway, what can you do for the girl?'

Michael's brooding eyes were still fixed on Sabastian's table. 'I don't know but I'm not leaving tomorrow. I'll catch next Thursday's boat and meet you in Brindisi.'

Wilkinson could not control the sweat on his face. 'One day, one week – what difference can it make to the girl? You've got to come, Mike – it's too bloody dangerous.' When he received no reply he went on desperately: 'What about your old man? He'll blow his top off when he hears of it.'

The muscles on Michael's face were as rugged and bleak as the Yorkshire fells in winter as he turned to Wilkinson. 'I don't care what he or anyone else thinks or does. I'm not leaving tomorrow.'

Early the following morning Cristina stood in the doorway of her father's shop, gazing anxiously down the piazza. She was waiting for Giuseppe who had left half an hour earlier for Carmillo's house, carrying in his pocket the five thousand six hundred lire she had managed to collect for him.

She saw him come out of an alley at last, hands thrust deep into his pockets and feet kicking dejectedly at the sunlit cobblestones. Her heart sank as she ran towards him.

'What did he say? Will he wait until the weekend for the rest?'

Giuseppe's sensitive face was sullen. 'Wait? He's worse than he was on Thursday – his wife must have been nagging at him. He says I've got until nine o'clock tonight, and if he doesn't have the money by then he's going straight to the police. He says he's got plenty of witnesses.'

She saw the same dread in his eyes that was in her own, and she swallowed a hard lump in her throat. 'Then we shall have to speak to Father now. There's nothing else we can do.'

He nodded without speaking and they walked slowly back to the shop, unconsciously dragging out time as much as possible. At the side entrance he turned to her. 'I know Maria will have to hear about it but we want to speak to Father alone first, don't we?'

She hesitated. 'I suppose so. But it won't be easy.'

He nodded at the shop door. 'You've got a key – you go inside and wait. I'll think of some excuse and bring him in. She shouldn't hear us in there.'

Cristina unlatched the door of the shop and closed it behind her. Inside it was very quiet, all shadows and sunbeams. The familiar musty smell came to her as she walked down the shop and paused at the counter. Two minutes later Carlo shuffled in, followed by Giuseppe. He was wearing his old black suit, newly-brushed and pressed for Mass. He opened his mouth to speak, then paused as Giuseppe put his fingers to his mouth and closed the house door.

'What is this?' he muttered, taking his cue and keeping his voice low. 'What are you two up to?'

Giuseppe threw a glance at Cristina. She hesitated, then approached Carlo. 'We've something to tell you, Father. Peppi had an accident on Thursday night and we're wondering if you can help him...'

Her voice faltered at Carlo's expression. Apprehension, fear, a dozen emotions were mixed in it as he turned fearfully to Giuseppe. 'What is it, Peppi? What have you done now?'

Sullenly, with hanging head, the boy told him. Carlo stared at him incredulously. 'You took another man's lorry... Do you realise what this could mean?'

Expecting recrimination, Giuseppe was even touchier when it came. 'Of course I know. Do you think me a fool?'

There had been a time when Carlo Delfano would have exploded in magnificent wrath when one of his children answered him back in such a fashion. Now his effort to kindle the old fires was pitiable.

'You have no sense of responsibility at all, Peppi. You drink with good-for-nothings, you laze about, and things like this keep on happening ... things we cannot afford.' His voice dropped fearfully. 'How much does Signor Carmillo want for the bicycle?'

Giuseppe's nerve failed him again and he threw another glance at Cristina. Her face was pale. 'He wants twenty thousand lire for it. And there is also some damage to the lorry...'

The air left Carlo's lungs like the wind from a punctured tyre. 'Twenty thousand lire! *Mamma mia!* But that is impossible. If I gave you all I had taken this week it would not come to that. And there is food to buy, bills to pay...'

She interrupted him hastily. 'I have managed to give him five thousand six hundred. And perhaps Pietro might be able to lend me a little more today. I could ask him...'

Carlo lifted his arms, dropped them. 'Old Pietro. A ferry boatman. What can he do? He is poorer than us.'

He stood grey-faced, staring at nothing. Cristina broke the silence. 'Father, Giuseppe needs at least fourteen thousand lire before tonight. Can you give it to him or not? We must know.'

Carlo put a shaking hand into the inside of his jacket and pulled out a notebook. He peered into it, then looked dully at her. 'When the bills are paid and the food is bought there is nothing, you understand. Less than nothing... I can only give it to him if I don't pay my creditors.'

Sympathy for him was like pain on her white face. 'I know how bad things are. But you'll have to give it to him, Father, otherwise it could be terribly serious...'

He turned to Giuseppe. 'Won't old Carmillo wait a few more days? Must he have the money today?'

Giuseppe shook his head. 'I've just been to ask him. He says he must have a new bike tomorrow: he uses it for his work. If he doesn't get the balance of the money by nine o'clock he's going straight to the police.'

'I shall have to speak to your stepmother first,' Carlo muttered. His words brought home to him the full dire implications of the affair and he turned back to Giuseppe. 'Isn't money hard enough to earn these days, Peppi, without your throwing it away? Why can't you pull yourself together and help us as Cristina does?'

A sensitive boy for all his shortcomings, Giuseppe had been feeling shame for longer than was comfortable. Carlo's recrimination gave it the escape valve it needed.

'Why can't *I* pull myself together! Am I the only one in the family, then, who spends his time drinking wine when he ought to be working?'

Carlo waved a frantic hand, too concerned at the noise the youth was making to pay much attention to his impudence. Cristina also tried to silence him but without success. His ashamed eyes stared resentfully at his father.

'Do you ever go round the island trying to bring business back to the shop? And what happens when we do earn money? *She* takes everything, except a miserable few lire. So what is there left but to drink wine and not think of the future?'

He swung round angrily. Cristina caught hold of his arm. 'Where are you going?'

'I don't know,' he muttered. 'Anywhere.'

'But you can't go yet. We haven't settled anything. Peppi! Come back...'

But the shop door slammed and Giuseppe was gone. Cristina made as if to run after him, then turned back to her father. At that moment Maria, her stepmother, appeared in the house doorway. Like Carlo she was already dressed for Mass, a stiff black costume and high-necked white blouse making her strong figure and hard, handsome face appear more formidable than ever. There was a rasp of suspicion in her voice as she stared at them.

'What's all this shouting? Where has Giuseppe gone? And why were the three of you shut in here like this?'

Carlo made one effort to speak and failed badly. In the painful silence the throb of a two-stroke diesel out in the bay could be heard clearly. Maria's eyes moved to Cristina. Conscious that every passing second was making matters worse Carlo made his plunge.

'It is nothing serious, Mamma... Only a little accident. We did not want to worry you with it until we had discussed it among ourselves.'

Her hard black eyes swung on him, pinning him like an insect to a board. 'An accident! What kind of accident?'

Carlo was visibly sweating. 'A bicycle was broken on Thursday night, Mamma. Peppi has to replace it and has asked if I can lend him the money...'

Storm clouds dropped at once over Maria's face. Her voice became ominously calm. 'And how did the bicycle get broken? Tell me that, Carlo.'

'As I say, Mamma, it was an accident...' Like Giuseppe before him Carlo looked at Cristina for help. Hesitantly she took over the story.

'It was a genuine accident, Maria. Guido was the real offender. He should never have dared Giuseppe to do it...' She went on to explain what had happened, doing her best to gloss over Giuseppe's folly.

She succeeded only in drawing some of the fire from Carlo. Maria's breathing was heavy with anger now. 'So, because your brother is a drunken fool and smashes up bicycles in a stolen lorry, we have to throw fourteen thousand lire into the gutter. Fourteen thousand lire – *Santa Maria,* it is madness. How will I find money for food?'

'It won't come out of the housekeeping money, Mamma,' Carlo assured her hurriedly.

She swung round on him. 'Housekeeping money or otherwise, what is the difference? It will bring us another step towards ruin. Already we owe money to almost every wholesaler and trader on the island. What kind of children did you give me? One gets himself drunk and into trouble every second week and throws our hard-earned money into the sea; the other offends the richest man on the island and loses us our business. What can one do with such creatures?'

Seeing that Cristina was going to be drawn into the affair Carlo made a gesture of protest. 'This is nothing to do with Tina, Mamma. She is not to blame.'

His defence of the girl was a psychological mistake, adding fuel to Maria's long-standing resentment. Her eyes snapped at him. 'Nothing, did you say? *Santa Maria*, it has everything to do with her. All our poverty comes from her stubbornness and her pride.'

It was a long time since Carlo had made such a spirited resistance to his wife and his expression showed the cost. 'No, Mamma. The fault is Sabastian's, not hers. Let us be fair.'

'Fair!' Maria twisted both her lips and his words to match her contempt. 'Sabastian wants something and he fights to get it. That is not unfair. That is life.'

Cristina gazed at her in astonishment. 'Not unfair? You don't think it's unfair of him to take away Father's trade because I won't marry him?'

Maria turned on her scornfully. 'What do you expect him to do? Give us a half-share in his fishing fleet?'

The girl's anger, although of a different quality, matched her own. 'I don't expect him to go around punishing innocent people just because he can't get what he wants. Only bullies do that!'

Maria's hand went on her hips. 'So, you think him a bully! You, a chit of a girl too young yet to know a man from a donkey.' Her contemptuous glance switched a moment to Carlo, touching him as a shoe touches a piece of dirt. 'When you're my age you'll appreciate a bit of spirit and fight in a man.'

'I hope there'll be other things I'll also appreciate,' Cristina said bitterly. 'Among them a little human kindness.'

Maria gave a rich exclamation of disgust. 'Those ideals of yours... When will you learn they are only for the rich, and today we are poor? And what have they brought you? I will tell you – loneliness. The girls on the island are jealous of you because you keep Sebastian from them, and the men are afraid even to talk to you. You are a fool, Cristina. It isn't even as if there was someone else you loved.'

Carlo made a last gallant foray from the huddled anonymity of his black suit. 'The poor child can never find anyone else when Sabastian puts his hooligans on them, Mamma.'

Maria shrugged. 'As I say, Sabastian is a man. He fights for what he wants. I don't blame him for that.'

'But Mamma, be fair to the girl. She does not love him. And surely love is more important than money...'

Maria's eyes were suddenly as bitter as unripe sloes.

'Is it, Carlo? For the woman... Are you quite sure?'

He suddenly looked very old and defeated and did not answer. She went to the door, swung round on them. 'It's easy for you two to talk so bravely of ideals when one of you spends his time bibbing wine in the piazza and the other works with nice clean hands in a school. I wonder how you'd feel if you had to haggle over every lire in the market as I do, trying to get food for your bellies. *Santa Maria;* you all make me sick.'

The door slammed, leaving behind a silence that was heavy with a hundred, unspoken regrets. Carlo, leaning against the counter, looked small and crumpled in the shadows. As Cristina turned to him he held out an unsteady hand. She broke into a run and clutched him tightly.

'Ah, *bambina mia,*' he muttered brokenly. 'What would I do without you?'

She pressed closer to him without speaking. The familiar smell of his old jacket, with its evocative childhood memories, had caught her without warning, making her feel suddenly vulnerable.

'She is right about me,' Carlo muttered. 'I am no good, not now. But she is so unfair to you. You give us all your money – without it we would all have been homeless long ago.'

Under his jacket she could hear the dull, heavy thud of his heart. He sighed again, then took hold of her face and turned it towards him. 'So like your mother, *cicci* ... Giuseppe resembles her too, but in Giuseppe there is something of me that spoils him. But you – you are all her. All her beauty and courage...'

Nostalgia was a dreamy undertone to his voice. The dust motes in the sunbeams seemed to pause like bright, suspended memories as she listened to him. 'Ah, *cicci;* that wonderful day in England when I first met her. It was so bright and splendid it must have slipped from heaven by mistake. I had never seen anyone as beautiful as she – one look at her and I was a king.' For a moment his voice was young and eager again. 'That was it, *cicci* – how I came to win her. Her inspiration made me worthy – she turned lead into gold.' Then his shoulders sagged as if the brittle bones beneath had suddenly snapped. 'Oh, *cicci mia,* why does life give us such wonderful gifts only to take them away?'

She was thinking of Pietro's words ... of earthenware jars broken by life and irreparable ... and emotion made it difficult for her to speak.

'You loved her so much, didn't you?' she whispered.

'Loved her, *cicci?* I worshipped her – she was my heaven on earth. When she died I went blind ... did stupid mad things. And that was wicked of me, because in her mercy she had left me her two most precious possessions. And how badly I have cared for them...'

'That isn't true. It's Sabastian who has

done this to you. You're not to blame.'

He shook his head slowly. 'No, *cicci*. That has finished me, it is true, but even before that I was starting to lose business. Maria and Giuseppe are right – I drink and drink and have become a defeated old man.' His hand groped for hers, gripped it tightly. 'But I have known great love, *cicci*, and because I am sober today I know what your mother's reply would have been. Oh, *cicci*, she would have lifted her proud head and said: "Never, never, never … no matter what happens, no matter if we starve…" And that is what you must promise me you will always say.'

She half-moved to speak, then pressed her cheek against his coat again. He put a hand under her chin. 'You don't say anything, *cicci*.'

She tried to smile. 'I've no intention of marrying him. You know that.'

'But you don't promise me. Why is that?'

She hesitated. 'I can't make a definite promise like that. No one knows what the future might hold.'

Carlo's voice was hushed. 'You don't like him, do you, *cicci*? Deep down underneath, I mean?'

She smiled at him. 'No. Not now.'

'Then why will you not promise me? I want your promise' – the shudder that ran through Carlo was like a sudden wind through a rotting tree. 'I am afraid that if things grow worse I may turn into a Judas one day and also try to persuade you. If ever that happens, *cicci*, come and tear your mother's photograph from my wallet because I shall no longer be worthy to carry it.'

She comforted him like a mother comforting a child. 'I've no intention of marrying Sabastian, so let's stop talking about it. This money for Giuseppe is much more urgent. What shall we do if Maria won't agree to giving it?'

Carlo, ever quick to change mood, had recovered himself now. He patted her thick glossy hair and even managed a sly wink. 'Don't worry – she feels the disgrace of being poor quite enough without wanting Giuseppe to be taken to court. By this afternoon I shall be able to give him the money. Fourteen thousand four hundred lire you said, *cicci?*'

She nodded. 'Yes. I had one thousand seven hundred lire, Pietro lent me one thousand four hundred and I managed to earn another two thousand five hundred yesterday showing the two Englishmen around the island.'

Carlo's voice was pathetically hopeful. 'Is there any chance of earning more?'

She knew nothing of Michael's decision to stay on and shook her head. 'No. They are leaving today for the other islands.'

'You said the lorry was damaged too, *cicci*.

Are its repairs included in this fourteen thousand four hundred lire?'

'No. Peppi says that will cost another four or five thousand...' Her voice quickened as Carlo's hand began rising again in despair. 'Don't worry about that. The lorry belongs to Sabastian, and as he's behind all this trouble he'll have to wait a few days. I shall see him and tell him he'll get the money on my next pay day.'

CHAPTER 8

Wilkinson opened his suitcase and took a clean handkerchief from it. As he slid it back under his bed he noticed the white-washed double room was empty. The door to the balcony stood open and he glanced through it. Michael was out there, leaning against the iron railing and staring across the piazza. Wilkinson hesitated a moment and then joined him.

A bell was tolling monotonously: the call to Mass from the small church in the Vicolo Stefano. Small groups of islanders were moving slowly across the piazza in answer to it: the men stiff and uncomfortable in their dark suits, the children equally subdued with their freshly-scrubbed knees and polished faces. Only the women, graceful in their veils, seemed at ease. Wilkinson jabbed his pipe at them.

'To look at 'em now you wouldn't think butter would melt in their mouths, would you?'

Michael nodded without speaking, and Wilkinson saw that his eyes were following a group of four people who had almost reached the entrance of the Vicolo Stefano. Two of them were middle-aged, one a youth, and the other a slim, veiled girl. Before they turned into the street the girl threw a quick nervous glance back. Wilkinson looked at Michael.

'That was Miss Delfano, wasn't it?'

Michael stared at him challengingly. 'Yes. Why?'

Wilkinson took a deep breath and tried again. 'Now look, Mike, you've got to be sensible about this. I know how you feel about the girl – she seems a nice kid and it gives anyone the needle to hear how this Cerone character is pushing her around. But face it – what good can you do by staying here a few more days?'

When he received no reply Wilkinson felt he might be gaining ground. 'Wherever you go in the world you find people in trouble, Mike. You'd love to help 'em, but you've got your own life to live... We've got a job to do for your father. You can't give it up just like that for a girl you've only known a couple of days.'

Michael stared at him moodily. 'Is the job all that important? Anyway, you don't need me to advise you about the other islands. You'll do the job quicker without me.'

'That's all very well, but what happens if your father hears what you've done? It's no use beating about the bush, Mike – everyone knows how things are between you both.'

'And you'll see he's tipped off if I don't come with you. Is that what you're saying?'

Wilkinson felt a burn of righteous indignation. 'I never said that. I'll keep it quiet if I can. But you know the odds are he'll phone through to Daco. What am I going to say if he asks to speak to you?'

'Tell him the truth. I'm not asking you to cover me.'

'But that could finish you – lose you your inheritance... Mike, for heaven's sake – what's the girl to you? You can't be in love with her – you've only known her a couple of days. And what good can you do by staying? If she's as nice a kid as I think, she won't want you to stay for fear of getting you into trouble.'

It was well-intentioned but had the wrong effect. Michael's hands tightened on the balcony rail. 'It's no use, Jack. I'm not leaving today.'

Wilkinson groaned, inwardly damning all

pig-headed Yorkshiremen. 'Mike, when that ship sails this afternoon you're here to stay until next Thursday. That's four days and nights, and it could seem an awful long time… Cerone isn't a fool – he'll know your reason for staying.'

Michael's voice was hard. 'No one's disputing that.'

'All right! So you're straight into it…' Wilkinson waved a hand at the blue harbour, at the pigeons strutting about in the sun below. 'Don't let all this picture-postcard stuff fool you, Mike. These island feuds aren't kids' quarrels. They can blow up like dynamite, particularly if foreigners interfere.' There was a great deal of good in Wilkinson and it was all in his voice now. 'Keep out of it, Mike, please. Come with me this afternoon.'

His concern, so obviously genuine, brought a sudden warmth to Michael's voice. 'I think you're exaggerating things a bit, Jack. Ten to one nothing will happen and I'll be bored stiff for four days. Stop worrying and come and have a beer with me.'

The afternoon was hot and sultry. Barefooted, sun-blackened children chased one another over the cobbles of the piazza or dived like young dolphins into the warm water. In the far corner of the harbour a crowd of islanders watched a water-polo match. Their shouts bruised the heavy summer air.

Michael sat alone in a corner of the verandah. His thoughts were mixed and moody, attempting to weigh the consequences of his decision in one moment, avoiding them in a flurry of impatience the next. Whatever happened he was staying, and there seemed little point in worrying about events that might never happen. Yet one worry kept recurring – the effect on his father. There was never any ambiguity about John Forbes – he had made it clear from the beginning that this was his son's last chance – and a direct disobedience of orders could well bring about the split neither of them desired. It was a thought that made Michael shift restlessly in his chair. The loss of an inheritance was one thing – a big thing but still a thing a man might one day look back on without regret. But the secret breaking of a lonely, stubborn old man's heart was another.

His moody eyes, trying to escape from his thoughts, caught sight of a girl in a blue frock moving away from the crowd watching the water-polo match. He recognised her graceful walk at once, and was rising from his chair when he saw a man detach himself from the crowd and follow her. He too was easily recognised – it was Sabastian wearing an emerald green shirt and a yellow scarf at his throat. Cristina swung sharply round as he caught up with her. They spoke for a moment and then continued walking towards the jetty.

Michael watched them, uncertain what to do. They were still too distant for their expressions to be seen, but he could see they were quarrelling. They halted at a group of stalls and here the quarrel appeared to come to a climax, Cristina turning abruptly away and making across the piazza for the hotel. Sabastian watched her for a moment and then returned to the crowd on the waterfront.

Michael rose and waved a hand. She saw him and half-broke into a run. He saw now that her face was pale and he crossed the verandah to meet her. She ran up the steps, one hand holding up her blue frock, her bright hair bobbing in the sunlight.

'Michael. I must talk to you…'

He led her to his table. In spite of her agitation her bare arms and cool frock brought a freshness to the sultry afternoon. He sat down opposite her.

'That was Sabastian you were talking to just now, wasn't it? I didn't know whether to interfere or not.'

'I'm glad you didn't. I wanted to see him – to tell him I would pay for the repairs to his lorry as soon as I could.'

'Did he say anything else?' he asked, watching her.

She nodded jerkily. 'Yes. That was why I

came straight across. He says you told him last night that you're not leaving today.'

'That's right,' he said quietly. 'I'm not.'

Her eyes were wide, frightened. 'But why? I had no idea. Yesterday afternoon I believed...'

'That was yesterday afternoon,' he said curtly. 'Since then I've changed my mind.'

She misunderstood his curtness and her voice faltered. 'It's none of my business, I know. But there is something I must tell you. Sabastian has got the ridiculous idea you are staying on because of me. I told him he must be crazy but he wouldn't listen to reason...'

He found deep satisfaction in saying the blunt words: 'He's not crazy. It's true.'

There was a short, stunned silence. Then her hushed voice: 'You can't mean it. You can't be serious.'

'I'm very serious.' His eyes crinkled at her. 'Don't look so frightened. You look as if you want me to go.'

'I do want you to go. It's terribly important that you go.' Then, afraid of being misunderstood, she said more than she intended. 'You mustn't think it is because I don't want to see you again. I think yesterday was the happiest day of my life...'

The unexpectedness of her confession made him stiffen, losing her her cause before she advanced it. 'It's because of Sabastian, Michael. He has just told me to warn you to go. And so you must go – for my sake. I couldn't bear it if anything happened to you.'

His moody face turned fierce. 'Warn me! Who the devil does he think he is to tell people what they shall do! I'm staying – as long as I like. You can tell him that.'

'But you don't understand, Michael… Some of his men will do anything for money and keep their mouths closed afterwards. It's true – you must believe it. He'll hurt any man who becomes friendly with me.'

There was a dryness in his throat at her confirmation of Wilkinson's warning. But his stubbornness was independent of his apprehension and grew in direct proportion to the threat. It showed in the muscles of his face, ridged like undersurf sand. 'I don't know about that, but I do know I'm not going on that boat this afternoon. Not if the whole damned island starts to threaten me.'

'If you do stay…' It was the hardest thing she had to say and she stumbled over it. 'If you do stay I shan't be able to see you, Michael. It will be the only way to keep you safe.'

His resentment spilled over and he gripped her wrist angrily. 'Now listen to me. You're tackling this thing the wrong way. It has to be fought and you need friends alongside you, not hiding to keep themselves out of trouble.' The anger in his voice startled her. 'To hell with Sabastian! Let's show him we're not afraid of him. That's the only way to handle bullies, big or small.'

Fearing for his safety, she was puzzled at the way her spirit was roused by his defiance, not realising it came from the same racial roots as his own. 'What are you suggesting we do?'

'Stay with me this afternoon,' he said eagerly. 'At least until we've seen Jack off on the boat. He's out shopping at the moment, then he has to pack. Until he's ready we'll sit out here in full view of the island and show Sabastian we don't give a damn for his advice.'

There was a glory in this recklessness, although every instinct told her it was summer madness and could not last. 'And what then?'

He grinned at her. 'Then we'll arrange to meet again this evening.'

CHAPTER 9

The local ferry was a small motor vessel, small enough to berth on the inside of the jetty. Michael and Cristina went as far as the gangway with Wilkinson. His heavy face was gloomy with foreboding as he took Michael's hand. 'Take care of yourself, Mike, for God's sake. Remember what I've told you and don't miss that mainland boat next Thursday whatever happens. I'll try to stall off the old man until then if I can.' Resentment was only half-concealed in his voice when he turned to Cristina. 'Goodbye, Miss Delfano. Thanks for your help.'

One of the crew took his suitcase on board. Wilkinson followed him and seated himself at the rear of the boat. A minute later the beat of the throbbing diesel grew louder, churning up the blue water. Michael waved a hand. ''Bye, Jack. Have a good trip. See you next Thursday.'

Wilkinson waved back but did not answer. They had a last glimpse of his worried face staring back at them before the motor vessel headed out into the bay. Islanders stopped waving to their friends and began drifting back along the jetty. Michael noticed their sidelong glances. He and Cristina had not walked ten yards before she turned to him.

'Your friend resented me. He believes I will get you into trouble.'

Michael shrugged. 'What does it matter? He's not my keeper.'

'It matters to me. He sees the danger too.'

'Jack sees danger in everything,' he told her impatiently. 'Stop worrying about it.'

The crowd around them thinned and they saw a group of four men standing alongside the stalls halfway down the jetty. As Cristina started Michael paid them more attention. One he recognised as the ferret-faced man who had been trailing Cristina on Friday night. The other three, although dressed as fishermen, were ugly enough to be a gangster's bodyguard. He glanced sharply at Cristina.

'Sabastian's men?'

She nodded, her voice breathless. 'Yes. They must have been watching to see if you sailed.' She turned to him urgently. 'Keep up with the rest of the people. Please don't fall behind.'

As they drew level with the men Mario showed his decayed teeth in a grin and spoke to Cristina. She did not answer him. The eyes of the four men then turned on Michael, subtly changed in expression. One of them said something to him in the island patois, flinging the words sharply like stones. He could not understand it but the rest of the group laughed. He saw Cristina's face turn pale and his jaw tightened.

'What did he say? Tell me.'

She would not answer, hurrying down the jetty instead. By the time they had reached the opposite side of the piazza his temper had cooled. 'Are you certain you won't have dinner with me tonight?'

'No. My family are expecting me.'

'Then I'll see you at eight as we arranged.'

All her fears had returned. 'We shouldn't,

Michael. You see how they are watching us.'

'Let's not go into all that again. You've already promised this evening to me. Where shall we go? Shall we stay in the hotel or go somewhere more quiet?'

Until she knew more of Sabastian's intention she wanted to keep Michael in the more populated part of the town. The piazza was always busy in the evenings but it was also a haunt of Sabastian's men... Her eyes lifted doubtfully. 'There is a bar in the Vicolo Palmo called the Pizzerina. It is a little more expensive than the others and so the fishermen do not use it. Do you know the street?'

'I think so. It runs off the Vicolo Stefano, doesn't it?'

'That's right. Go alone and I will meet you there.'

When he protested she shook her head determinedly. 'No, Michael; we go alone or I shall not come. Keep away from side streets when you go, and do your best not to be followed. I'll do the same and will be there at eight. *Arrivederci.*'

As Michael walked slowly back along the cobbled pavement he saw the four men were now standing on the opposite side of the piazza. The skin on his back felt oddly tight as he mounted the steps of the verandah and entered the hotel.

The sky over the bay was like a red wound

when Michael left the hotel that evening. The festivity of the Sunday evening had not yet got under way although the filling pavement tables gave ample warning of it. He could see no one he recognised as he started down the piazza for the Vicolo Stefano, but with his limited knowledge of Sabastian's men he knew this meant little. His only hope of detecting pursuers if they were in attendance was to catch them in the act of pursuit.

At the entrance of the Vicolo Stefano he turned. A few yards behind him walked three cloth-capped men whose animated conversation made them appear innocent enough. Behind them were a youth and a girl, lost in each other's eyes. Across the piazza people were less easy to identify, being only moving silhouettes against the red sunset. A narrow side street branched off on his right, rising in irregular flights of cobbled steps. He hesitated a moment, then slipped into it. He walked quickly for thirty yards or so, saw no one following him, and turned left into a narrow alley. It led him through two blocks of shabby tenements, out into a lane, and finally into the cobbled street of the Vicolo Palmo. It was lined with shops, one staggered above the other to follow the rise of the hillside.

He recognised the Pizzerina, fifty yards up the street, by the tables out on the pavement. He paused outside it and gazed through the open door. The bar was at the far end with small tables flanking either wall. Two wrought-iron screens made a pretence of dividing the room in two. On the near side two elderly men were sunk deep in conversation at a table by the window. On the far side, on stools alongside the bar, two men and two girls were laughing and talking: young married couples by their appearance.

Taking what cover was offered Michael chose a table directly behind the left-hand screen. As he sat down he noticed the chatter from the young couples behind him had ceased. A sallow-faced bartender, dog-dismal behind a sagging black moustache, came round the bar for his order. He asked for a glass of Moscato, his ears cocked at the silence behind him. As he lit a cigarette the chatter came back and he slowly relaxed. He glanced at his watch. It was seven minutes to eight.

Three middle-aged men entered and took the table opposite him. Their stares at him contained no more than the islanders' natural curiosity towards an outsider, and after a bottle of wine was placed on their table they paid him no more attention.

Cristina was only a minute late, pausing as he had paused in the open doorway. She was wearing a grey cardigan over a green, full-skirted print frock. Her face was flushed from hurrying and her eyes nervous as they darted around the bar. Then she saw him and came quickly forward.

The chatter behind Michael stopped dead again. Awareness of it gave his voice a certain embarrassment as he went forward to greet her. 'Hello. You are a punctual person. Practically dead on time.'

She was nervously eyeing the party of young people at the bar as he offered her a seat. 'Was everything all right?' she whispered. 'Did anyone see you?'

'I don't think so – I was very careful coming here. What about you?'

'One of them was watching the house. But I pretended I was going up to the school hall – I often go there in the evenings when the children are rehearsing a concert – and he didn't follow me very far.' She turned, gazed anxiously at the wrought-iron partition behind her. 'Will they be able to see us through this when it becomes dark outside?'

Like himself she was watching to see if anyone left the bar now Michael's purpose there was established. When no one moved and the chatter began rising again they both began to relax. After she had half-finished a glass of wine Michael drew her into talking about herself, for there were still many gaps in his knowledge of her. Gradually, as often as not by her hesitations and omissions as by her words, he learned more about the slow decay of her father under financial pressure, her stepmother's hostility, and the slow corrosion of her brother. Through her story, like a golden thread holding together a shredding garment, he traced her efforts to prevent the disintegration of her family, and his admiration deepened by the minute.

Before she finished the short Mediterranean twilight was over and dusk had fallen in the cobbled street outside. Most of the empty tables had filled by this time, but none of the newcomers had betrayed more than an evanescent interest in them. The melancholy barman came out from behind his counter with a lighted taper. As he went round the bar lighting wall candles a young guitarist appeared in the doorway. He had a short beard, a boyish face, and wore a red sash like a cummerbund around his slim waist. He walked down between the tables, pausing near Michael and Cristina. He plucked the guitar once and the chatter in the room died as if a switch had been thrown. In a mellow, pleasant voice he began singing a Neapolitan love song.

During the song Michael watched Cristina. In the soft candlelight her eyes were star-bright and her cheeks as smooth as a moss rose. She noticed his gaze, smiled at him and a laugh seemed to rise from him like a bubble from champagne.

'You're a beautiful girl, Cristina. Quite astonishingly beautiful.'

Happiness was a crimson flame that leapt

up from her glossy neck to her cheeks. He had to lean forward to hear her whisper. 'Whatever happens, Michael, I want to thank you for all this. I'd forgotten what it was like to be so happy...'

She turned abruptly away, but not before he noticed tears glistening in her eyes. His feelings defied analysis. There was a tenderness in him as soft as a woman's lips, and yet underneath it, like the boiler fires of a moonlit ship, a dark anger towards Sabastian glowed sullenly.

The guitarist moved away from them into the front half of the bar. He sang a second song, made his collection, and then departed. Neither Michael nor Cristina noticed the last backward glance he threw them from the doorway before he went. The last barriers of formality between them were down, and in their eagerness to learn more about one another they were as talkative as children. In their happiness they forgot danger, and the shock when it came seemed the more brutal.

Michael noticed the men first, crowding into the bar doorway. They were the four who had been on the jetty that afternoon, three of them in blue-and-white striped vests, the fourth, Mario, in a loud American chequered shirt and narrow teddy-boy trousers. His small eyes were on them, beady and exultant. Seeing Michael's expression Cristina swung sharply round. Her cry was one of pure agony. 'Michael! They've found us! Oh, *Santissima Madonna…*'

They came down the bar like grinning wolves. Mario leaned over the three middle-aged men sitting at the opposite table and said something in his harsh, staccato voice. The men showed instant alarm, two of them rising at once and leaving their glasses of wine. The third showed some resistance until Mario showed his decayed teeth and said four words to him. Then he too clutched his hat and followed his companions from the bar.

Laughing the men sprawled into the chairs, drinking the wine left on the table. The two young couples at the bar left their stools and hurried out, throwing startled glances back over their shoulders. Mario grinned across at Cristina, then thumped on the table and shouted for more wine. There was fear in the eyes of the thin barman as he hastened to bring them a bottle. Wine slopped over the table as Mario filled the glasses. He turned, lifted his glass to Cristina, and said something in the island patois that brought a roar of obscene laughter from his companions.

Michael saw her cheeks flame with anger, then go deathly pale. 'What did he say?' When she did not answer his voice gritted with fury. 'What did the little swine say? I want to know.'

Fear was running like a floodtide in her eyes. 'You mustn't take any notice of them. That's what they want.'

He knew that well enough, but rage was thrusting his reason aside. Mario raised his glass again, this time at him, and shouted something that brought another obscene laugh from the three other toughs. Cristina's face was ashen now. She tugged at his arm. 'We must go, Michael. At once. Please come with me.'

He knew she was right, but rising to leave was like tearing his flesh. As he followed her a foot came out, making him stumble. Fury swung him round. For a moment the laughter at the table hushed at his expression. Then it burst out loudly again as he followed her into the street.

Her voice was frantic. 'I must go straight home, Michael. Otherwise it will be too dangerous for you.'

Every obstinate, dogged nerve in his body shouted its protest. 'No; we're not giving in. To hell with them. We'll go round to the hotel and have a drink there.'

He still had much to learn. Before they had gone ten yards down the street Mario's men were on them, reinforced by two other cloth-capped toughs. The six men formed a chain across the narrow street in front of them, linking arms and chanting a song.

Growing like a maddened bulldog Michael

was going to barge his way forward when Cristina caught hold of him. 'No! That's what they want...' When she saw he was still going her voice turned desperate. 'I shan't see you again if you fight them. I mean it, Michael.'

He turned his black, enraged face towards her. 'Then what are we supposed to do? Stand here like fools while they make fun of us?'

'No; I'll go on alone... Yes, I must. They won't harm me and then they'll leave you alone too. It's the only way, Michael...' She was sobbing as she ran up to Mario. 'If I go home will you leave my friend alone?'

His voice, garlic-smelling, repeated her words mockingly. "Will you leave my friend alone, Mario..." You're the one who'd better leave your friend alone, Cristina Delfano.' He broke arms with the man on his right to make a gap for her. 'Go on, then – and go straight home.'

She threw back a last agonised glance. 'I'm sorry, Michael. But it's the only thing I can do for you...'

The laughing, chanting men closed in a circle around Michael, hiding her from his sight. For a moment relief that she was safe held back his anger. Then it blazed up again; he let out a snarl and shouldered his way forward. Two men caught hold of him and threw him back across the circle. Another arm thumped him in the back and sent him stumbling forward again. Their laughter made the air fetid with the fumes of wine and garlic. They linked arms again and began doing a grotesque ring-a-roses around him, still chanting the same song. Another arm pushed him and fury burst in his brain like a bomb. He lashed out and felt the solid, satisfying thud of knuckles against flesh. A man cursed and stumbled back from the circle. The laughter loudened but with a harsher, more threatening ring. Another arm pushed him violently forward, a foot made him stumble and fall. Then Mario shouted an order and he suddenly found himself lying alone in the dust of the badly-lit street.

He picked himself up and stumbled down the cobbled steps, making for the Vicolo Stefano. There was no sign of Cristina there and he ran for the piazza. He saw she had vanished and slowed down to a walk.

Men and women stared at his black, raging face and his dusty clothes as he pushed his way through the stalls and the crowded tables to her father's shop. A solitary light was shining in a window above it. He thought of her agony in the lonely room and there was murder in his heart. As he stood there a low laugh came from the dense shadows near the shop. He ran forward, searching viciously among them, but could find no one he knew. At last he was forced to return to his hotel. Ignoring the greeting of a porter in the entrance he tramped upstairs to his room and threw himself on the bed. It was minutes before his harsh breathing eased, and even then attacks of rage like ague shivered his body as he lay staring at the shifting lights in the window.

CHAPTER 10

Pietro saw the broad-shouldered, compact Englishman approaching him and winked a satisfied eye at a pigeon squatting on a nearby bollard. It was early Monday morning, and the old fisherman was sitting on a wooden crate at the edge of the jetty repairing a net. He lowered his head pretending to be lost in his task.

Michael stopped alongside him. 'Good morning.'

Pietro peered up, pulled the evil-smelling pipe from is mouth. *'Buon giorno, signor. What can I do for you?'*

'The other day you told me you were a good friend of Cristina's – the only one on the island she could trust. I've come to see if you'll help me.'

The directness of the request made the old man nod with fierce satisfaction. 'After what happened last night I wondered if you'd have the good sense to come to me, signor.'

'You've heard about it, then?'

'I heard this morning.' Pietro's growl was deep and fierce. *'Per Bacco,* I could slit the throats of the dogs that did it.' He leaned forward anxiously. 'Is the *piccinina* upset? Have you seen her since?'

'I tried to see her when she was going to school this morning. But we were being watched and she was too afraid to talk to me.'

Once more Pietro took in the grim stubbornness of the younger man's face. 'You're not afraid of them, then, signor?'

He noted with satisfaction the tightening of Michael's jaw. 'I'm not particularly happy about their attention, if that's what you mean. But I'm damned if I'm going to stop seeing her. That's why I've come to you. I wondered if you know of any place where I could safely meet her. Preferably outside the town. I don't see any way of avoiding them here.'

Pietro eyed him thoughtfully. He leaned forward again, pipe in hand. 'First I must ask you one thing, signor, because the *piccinina* is more to me than if she were my own daughter. You told me you were leaving on Sunday with your friend – you did not leave and I know the reason for it as well as Sabastian Cerone knows it. So now tell me, signor – do you mean well to my little *piccinina?* Because if you do not' – and the old pipe sliced before Michael's throat like a knife – 'you will have a far worse enemy on this island than Cerone.'

He saw a black cloud of resentment settle over Michael's face. 'What the devil do you mean? Of course I mean well to her.'

Pietro sat back on his box. His great laugh sent the nearby pigeon flying for its life. *'Per Bacco,* lad, I like you. You have anger and spirit, and a face like a granite cliff into the bargain. I will help you all I can.' His voice turned thoughtful. 'You want a quiet place where you can talk to her in safety... If I had a home you could meet there, but I live in a pension with four old men who would cackle like geese...'

'The town's no use anyway – they'll always find us. Don't you know of any place outside it where no one goes in the evenings?'

There was the sound of sandpaper on wood as Pietro rubbed his chin. 'You realise the danger is greater in lonely places, signor.'

'Surely they wouldn't do her any harm?'

'Not her. You are the one who has to be careful.'

'I'll take my chances if you'll find a place for us.'

Pietro nodded, rubbed his chin again. 'First the *piccinina* must agree to go. Have you asked her yet?'

'I haven't had a chance. I thought you

could go into the shop and ask for me.'

Pietro watched him closely. 'Why don't you go in yourself?'

'I don't think she would like that. Her father is in enough trouble already – I don't want to drag him into more if I can help it.'

Pietro nodded, well-satisfied. He weighed up the pros and cons. If the thing he wanted above all else was to be achieved some risks had to be taken… He spat down to the jetty. 'All right, signor; I will ask her for you. Now – a place to meet. It is not easy – the island is too full of people.' He lifted his grizzled head and nodded at the cliffs at the south side of the bay. 'Over there is a small cove – I know it because the seaweed beds are good and the octopus grow fat on crayfish there. Tina knows it too – she has sometimes gone out with me.'

Michael's voice was eager. 'It sounds promising. How do I find it?'

'It is about three kilometres from Veronia. It cannot be seen from the cliff top – it is small and the cliffs overhang at that point. Also the bushes are dense. But out at sea is a rock shaped like a turtle. When you see the rock opposite you, you walk on another hundred metres until the cliff shelves. There you will find a path – take it and it will lead you back through the bushes into the cove.' He paused. 'When must I arrange this meeting? For tomorrow evening?'

'Couldn't it be tonight?'

Pietro shook his head. 'On Monday afternoons Tina takes the children to the beach and in the evening there is a concert rehearsal… It will have to be tomorrow, signor. Shall I ask her to be there at seven o'clock?'

Michael, disappointed at the delay, nodded. 'As early as she can come. I shall be there from six-thirty onwards.'

It was a rare thing for Pietro's fierce old eyes to show anxiety but they showed it now. 'You will have to be very careful going there, signor. Tina should have no trouble – she often goes for an evening walk along the cliffs, and if she goes alone they will probably not follow her far. But if they have seen you go that way earlier they will be after her like a pack of hunting dogs.' He spat his disgust over the timbered coping of the jetty. 'It would happen I have promised to work in the evenings this week, or I would come out and keep guard for you.'

'There's no need for that. All I have to do is drop a hint in the hotel that I'm going to Proccio for the evening and leave the town in that direction. When I'm out of sight I'll double back to the cove and wait there until Cristina comes.' The doubt on the old man's face made Michael impatient. 'Don't worry about me. I had two years in the Army in Malaya – I know how to move around without being seen.'

134

Pietro scowled down at his pipe, pressed down the hot tobacco with a calloused finger. Then, as his eyes lifted up to Michael, a great, contemptuous laugh boomed out of him. *'Per Bacco;* what is the matter with me? For years I have prayed for a man who was not afraid of these mongrels. And when he comes I dither and doubt like an old woman... I will see Tina this evening as soon as she returns home from school. And then I will come round to the hotel...' The old fisherman's eyes suddenly narrowed. 'No, wait... Someone will be watching us now, and if they see me go to the shop and then to your hotel they may put two and two together. It will be better if I phone you at the hotel. About eight o'clock, signor.'

'Don't let her say no. Tell her there's nothing to be afraid of and that I must see her.'

Pietro grinned. 'I'll tell her that the cocky young cub who wants to see her is quite confident he can flatten half a dozen of Sabastian's mongrels with one swipe of his paw if necessary. That ought to ease her mind.' As Michael grinned back he went on: 'What are you going to do today?'

Michael motioned at the green cliffs across the bay. 'I might take a walk out there and make sure I can find the cove.'

Pietro's bushy eyebrows came together thoughtfully. 'Yes; with her at school you should be safe enough. But I would not stay out after dark.'

'I won't. I have to be back at the hotel before eight o'clock in any case to get your message.'

'You shall get it, signor. *Arriverderci.*' There was affection in Pietro's eyes as he gazed at the broad, receding back of the young Englishman.

Michael found the cove that afternoon without difficulty. Just over two miles along the cliffs he came opposite a rock white with guano and shaped like a huge turtle. Here the cliffs jutted out like a bearded chin, hiding the beach below. He continued along the cliff path and a minute later reached a point where a rock fall had made the cliff shelve. A narrow, overgrown path showed here, running downwards and back towards the invisible cove.

He gazed around him carefully. He was in a slight hollow, and with the empty hillside covering his back he felt certain he was unobserved. Quickly he jumped down to the path and pushed his way through the dense bushes.

The sagebush was in seed and pollen rose like dust around him. Through the branches of the she-oaks the bright blue sea shone like porcelain. A linnet leapt from a tree in fright and sped seawards like a green dart. The path checked its descent for a moment and led him over a saddle that connected an eroded promontory with the main cliff face. Then the descent continued, and through the branches of a bamboo he could see the cove ahead.

It was no more than forty yards in length, a narrow strip of beach bounded by rocks at one end and the eroded promontory at the other. He followed the path down until his feet sank into the yellow sand. He saw Pietro was right: the beach could only be over-looked from the promontory and, awkward of access as it was, they would have to be more than unlucky if a chance observer appeared on it the following evening.

There were a few traces of human visi-tation in the cove – a rusted tin lying among the bushes, an empty lemonade bottle half-buried in the sand – but nothing to suggest it was visited frequently. He wandered over to the rocks at the far end and sat down. The waves were small, splashing white among the rocks and rustling the pebbles. He lit a cigarette, wondering with sudden uneasiness if Pietro would be successful in his mission. The thought made him glance at his watch. It was barely four-thirty – he still had three and a half hours to pass before Pietro was due to phone. The thought depressed him – he was not looking forward to spending an evening alone in the seedy hotel.

With the breach in his mind once made

other depressing thoughts followed quickly into it. What exactly was he trying to achieve in seeing Cristina...? He remembered Wilkinson had asked him the same question. What result could come from another meeting other than a bitter-sweet hour together? It appeared she would never leave her father to face Sabastian alone, and he could not stay on the island longer than Thursday. Then was it wise to stir and tamper – perhaps even to raise hope only to let it fall? Would she not be worse off in every way if he kept seeing her until Thursday and then sailed away leaving her alone once more?

He rose and walked restlessly back along the beach, feeling the need to use his body to escape from his fretting mind. As his eyes fell on the eroded promontory ahead he suddenly thought of the Grotto of Tiberius. It was along this stretch of cliffs and could not be far away. Since Cristina had told him the legend the cave had held a fascination for him, and this was an excellent chance to see it at close quarters. He glanced at the sea. An exposed shelf of hard sand and seaweed-matted rocks suggested the tide was low – conditions for climbing down to the Grotto should be ideal. He hesitated no longer and started back up the path, conscious of an odd excitement.

The cliff top was still deserted when he reached it five minutes later. He topped the slight rise ahead and a magnificent vista of green cliffs and glossy blue sea stretched ahead of him. He walked quickly, his powerful body making little of the undulating path, and in less than fifteen minutes was in sight of the massive headland, jutting out into the sea like a cruel face with the Grotto a rapacious mouth below.

The cliff looked sheer and unscalable, but remembering what Cristina had said he crossed the thick neck that joined the headland to the main cliff face. Here erosion had bitten into the side of the neck like an ulcer, making a descent to the rocks below possible to an agile climber. He started down and was soon standing on one of the rock terraces that ran round the base of the headland.

He paused a moment. The tall cliffs trapped the heat of the sun, and his shirt was soaked and clinging to his body. He removed it and tied the sleeves around his neck before working his way round towards the Grotto.

As he went he noticed the sudden peculiar greenness of the sea. Progress was not difficult, however: the waves were a good ten feet below him, and although they made a hard slapping sound against the rocks they did nothing to deter him. Coaxing him onwards, perhaps – restraining themselves... He smiled at the grotesqueness of the thought.

A few minutes later he was standing at the mouth of the Grotto. It was much larger than he had imagined, a gaping entrance with a twelve-foot-wide gully through which the sea heaved and sucked with sounds that were oddly obscene. Alongside the deep gully a wide rock ledge ran back into the Grotto, with a knife-edge demarcation line between the brilliant sunlight outside and the darkness within. With the sun hot on his naked shoulders he found himself hesitating before it, vague misgivings tugging him back like hands. Impatiently he stepped forward, and instantly he was in another world where everything was dark and cold and had a smell that was not of the sea.

CHAPTER 11

The Grotto was huge inside with a high dome and walls that receded back into the shadows. As Michael's eyes became accustomed to the gloom, muted colours began to appear: the peculiar greenness of the eddying water, the brown scraps of seaweed cast up at the rocky edges of the gully, the ancient, lichen-stained walls. The floor was grey with guano, and looking up he could imagine seeing the huddled shapes of bats sleeping high up in the mysterious dome.

He walked deeper into the Grotto, and the

hollow echo of his footsteps sounded over the splash and suck of the waves. The deep gully fascinated him: he followed it back and saw it ran into a large, half-submerged hole in the rear of the cave. The hole was no wider than the gully, making it impossible to tell how far it ran back into the cliff, but he saw it was the cause of the obscene noise the waves made as they swelled forward into it and then sucked back. As he stood there he became conscious of the strange smell again. It seemed to come and go: the smell of decay and wet earth, of the newly-turned grave... The morbidity of the thought shocked him. He walked back a few yards, found a rock shelf near the edge of the gully and sat watching the restless water.

The gully was deep and oddly sinister. Fanciful thoughts came to him as he stared into it. The long-dead lovers, victims of the power and cruelty of ancient Rome, huddled together in the cold Grotto at night ... dreaming of a golden world where they were free to walk together in the sun and the wind and the rain. Pressed together for comfort, and not seeing the long arms that rose one night like sea serpents from the dark gully and seized them. Their screams for one another, their terror as they were dragged mercilessly down into the deep, green water...

Something of their agony had been left in the Grotto. In spite of the heat outside it sank into the body like an icy chill. As Michael went to the entrance and glanced back the appearance of the Grotto seemed to change. Now the writhing water in the gully became an ancient sea-god, the dark Grotto was its lair. Shaking his head at his imagination he stepped out into the sunlight.

It was a return to the present century and a return to life. The sun wrapped a warm blanket around his chilled body. Beyond the green water around the headland the sea was a great stretch of glossy blue enamel with waves as white as lace as they broke on the rocks. A cormorant sped by, its tiny black head craned down in its search for fish. The smell of salt and seaweed made him breathe deeply.

He made his way back round the rock terraces and began the steep climb to the cliff top. As he climbed the strong feeling he was being watched grew on him. He paused and stared around. He could see no one, but the rocks and thick bushes above could have concealed a hundred watchers. Ten minutes later he reached the cliff top, hot again and breathless from his exertions. He had seen no one and the cliffs were deserted. It was cooler up there – a slight breeze was blowing off the land – and as his shirt was now dry he pulled it on before starting back to Veronia.

Something of the mood he had felt in the Grotto was still with him, and when he reached the cliff from which Cristina had first shown it to him he glanced back. Once again he was impressed by the startling resemblance of the headland to an out-thrust cruel face and the peculiar hard greenness of the water surrounding it. He had a feeling almost of relief when the undulating path finally hid it from his sight.

He returned to Veronia by the more direct cliff path instead of the inland road. A lemon haze lay on the horizon, and the sun had sunk behind it by the time he made his way along the waterfront towards the piazza. Its half a dozen cranes were standing idle and two barges were yawing against their fenders. The smell of frying fish from one of them reminded him he had not eaten since noon. Two of the crew were sitting in the bows, smoking their pipes. Both glanced at him as he walked by, but there was no malice in their curiosity.

He reached the piazza and started across it. It was crowded with young men and girls parading about and eyeing one another, and he remembered with amusement a comment of Wilkinson's. 'On the islands they always call the piazza "La Tonnara", Mike. La Tonnara is the big net into which the tunny fish are led during the June migrations. It means the Death Chamber – where the poor fish finally meet their end – so you'll get the general idea…' A typical example of Wilkinson's mordant sense of humour, Michael thought, with sudden affection.

No one appeared to be paying him any particular attention, and yet as he crossed the cobblestones towards the hotel he felt he was being watched all the time. He glanced at the hardware shop as he passed by, hoping to catch a glimpse of Cristina. Faded grey blinds in the shop windows, like the eye membranes of a bird, showed it was closed. He looked at the bedroom window above, then remembered she would not yet have left the school.

A young, pale-faced boy called Gino, the son of the manager, was at the desk when Michael entered the hotel. Telling the youth he was expecting a phone call Michael went upstairs to his room. His cold shower and change of clothes took less than twenty minutes, by eight o'clock he had eaten and was waiting impatiently in the lounge. He had smoked two cigarettes and was halfway through a third when he heard the telephone ring. He was out in the hall before the youth had put the receiver down.

'Is it mine?'

'*Si, signor.*'

The phone stood on a rickety table near the desk. Conscious that he had awakened the youth's curiosity, Michael kept his voice low. 'Hello, Forbes here.'

There was no mistaking Pietro's harsh

voice. 'Signor the Englishman. This is Pietro. Can you hear me well?'

'Yes: I can hear you. What's your news?'

'I saw her a few minutes ago, signor. It is all right – she will see you as arranged.'

Michael felt his muscles slacken in relief. 'Good man. That's a bottle of wine I owe you.'

Pietro's great laugh made the phone crackle in protest. 'Two bottles, signor. She fought hard – she thought it was too dangerous for you. It was only when I told her that otherwise you would come round to her house that she agreed.'

'What time will she be there?' At that moment Michael remembered the pale-faced youth and glanced up quickly. The boy had been watching him: now he was staring down at a paper-back on the desk. Pietro's voice grated in the receiver.

'As near seven as she can, signor. She asks you to be very careful. If anyone sees you near the cove you must go back immediately. She will understand if you are not there.'

'All right,' Michael told him. 'And thanks again for your help.'

He hung up the receiver and glanced again at the desk. The pale-faced youth felt his stare and looked up. He gave an uncertain smile.

'Is everything all right, signor?'

A hell of a question, Michael thought with a sudden snap of anger, when you and everyone else on the island might be spying on me... Then, helped by the memory of his rendezvous the following day, he shrugged off the mood. Things had to be kept in perspective, and at the worst he had given away no details of time or place...

'Yes; everything's fine, thanks.' He moved a few steps from the phone and turned back to the youth. 'Get one of your chaps to bring me a cold beer, will you? I'll be outside on the verandah.'

'*Si, signor.* At once.' There was nothing in the boy's expression to arouse any misgivings as he jumped willingly from his stool and hurried down the hall.

The following day Michael had another phone call with equally dramatic possibilities. It came in the late afternoon after a day that had seemed impossibly long. It was from his father.

John Forbes had no patience for preliminaries and made none. He came to his point as abruptly as a bull tackling a five-barred gate.

'That you, Mike? I've just been speaking to Wilkinson. He tells me you've stayed behind in Veronia. Why? What's the game?'

Michael started cautiously. 'Didn't you ask Wilkinson?'

'Of course I did. But the old devil hedged, said he wasn't sure. Sounded as if he were trying to cover you. What's going on, Mike?'

'Does anything have to be going on? Jack didn't need me to look those islands over – you know that. In fact he'll do the job quicker without me.'

John Forbes' grunt of impatience might have come from across the hall instead of far-off Leeds. 'That's no answer. I thought we'd at last come to an understanding, you and me. And that understanding was that if you came into the business you'd do things my way – do as you're told. Right?'

Michael's face was grim now. 'Go on.'

'I sent you out on this trip under Wilkinson. It wasn't much more than a holiday really – all you had to do was keep your eyes open and learn all you could. But I told you to stay with Wilkinson because he knows his Italy and can teach you a lot. And you haven't. Why?'

'I've already told you. There wasn't any need for me to visit the other islands with him.'

'That's no answer. I said you had to stay with him and you haven't. You're hedging, Mike – holding something back. What is it?'

Underneath the anger in the blunt voice was an unmistakable plea. 'Give me a reason, lad – I don't want a final break any more than you do. But, by golly, if you act proud and pig-headed you're still out – right on your ear…'

x

147

Michael glanced around him. Gino, the pale-faced youth, was again at the desk. Perhaps he couldn't speak much English, but Michael wasn't certain. And he thought of the impossibility of explaining over the phone something he hadn't been able to explain to Wilkinson ... something he couldn't yet explain fully to himself...

'I can't tell you, Dad – not yet. It isn't that I won't – I just can't. But I promise to explain everything that's happened when I get back.'

John Forbes was not diverted as easily as this. 'I want to know now, Mike. Stop hedging. Is it some woman?'

His choice of words and his tone were unfortunate, stirring Michael's temper. 'What if it was? Wouldn't it be my business?'

He regretted his defiance the moment he made it. There was a dull ache in his stomach as he listened to the result.

'No, by golly it wouldn't – not when you're doing a job for me. I've warned you before – you obey my orders like everyone else or out you go. This is your final warning, Mike. On Thursday, woman or no woman, you meet Wilkinson in Brindisi. Otherwise you'll be out on your own. And I won't have any second thoughts this time, m'lad. It'll be for quits, final.'

There was no opportunity to reply. Only a sharp click at the other end, followed by a hurt, angry silence that carried its own message. As he went upstairs to change his clothes for the walk to the cove Michael realised he felt slightly sick.

CHAPTER 12

Before leaving the hotel Michael told the pale-faced youth that he was taking a walk to Proccio and would not require dinner as he would be spending the evening there. He set off in the direction of the village, climbing up the cobbled street that passed near Cristina's school and on up the hillside until Veronia fell away from sight. Then he turned south, following tracks that he hoped would eventually bring him to the dirt road that encircled the island. It was a hot, roundabout route on which he was inevitably noticed by some of the peasants still toiling in the vineyards. This he had expected, but in assessing his chances had gambled that his single presence could hardly be of sufficient value for an informer to pass on. He had to be somewhere on the island, so his argument ran, and if he appeared unhurried enough they would only assume he was taking a walk.

He found the dusty road without difficulty and followed it until it veered round a hill towards the cliffs. A quarter of a mile further on he encountered it again as it looped back inland. He followed it for another two hundred yards and finally abandoned it altogether for a narrow path that led up the hill on his right. From the hilltop he took bearings on the cove and started down, moving cautiously now through the thick vegetation. Once down the hill he kept off the cliff path until he was opposite the point where the cliff shelved. He made certain the cliffs were deserted before running quickly over the path and leaping for cover in the bushes below. In another five minutes he was walking safely along the yellow sand of the cove.

It was nearly a quarter past seven when he heard the distant rustle of bushes. Throwing his cigarette aside he ran eagerly back along the path. Through the bushes he caught sight of her hair, the slanting sun making it look like a golden, dancing flower.

She saw him, hurried forward, and stumbled over a tree root. He found his arms around her, with her hair like warm silk against his face. For a moment she lay still against him, only her quick breathing moving her body. Then she lifted her head anxiously. 'Is it safe for you, Michael? Did anyone see you come?'

He checked her fears with his lips. It was their first kiss and happiness was a delirium in them both. They kissed again, and their bodies seemed to become a part of the summer evening around them, light and glowing and vitally alive.

She checked him at last and they went down together to the cove. They found a seat on the rocks at the far end and there she turned to him reproachfully. 'You never answered me. Are you certain no one saw you come?'

He took hold of her hand. 'Quite certain. Stop worrying about it.'

She let him kiss her again, but now he felt a change of mood in her. 'What is it, darling? What are you worrying about?'

She was gazing at the eroded promontory at the opposite end of the cove and at the thick wall of bushes behind them. 'This is too dangerous for you. It would be a trap if anyone saw us. I shouldn't have agreed to come.'

He smiled, trying to allay her fears. 'Pietro said you put up quite a fight.'

She was anxious that he should understand. 'It wasn't that I didn't want to come … for myself. I'm frightened for you, Michael. If Sabastian found out we were alone here it would be much worse than our being together in town. That's why I'm so afraid.'

The damped-down fires of anger in him began glowing again. 'You shouldn't always have to be worried and afraid. That was one of the reasons I wanted to see you tonight.' He took her hands, turned her to face him. 'Listen to me. I want you to leave the island.

On Thursday there's a boat to the mainland – I want you to sail on it with me. Don't worry about the fare – I'll see to all that. Just come with me and get away from this prison.'

It was said and he was glad of it, and yet what would happen afterwards he did not know. He had saved no money of his own, and she would need help until she found work. Also there was her family – he knew she would never leave unless some satisfactory provision were made for them. He had tried to work something out during the long hours of waiting, but always his thoughts had jolted painfully into the dour, inflexible figure of his father. Without him there was no work and no money, and without these he could only help her to reach the mainland. But there was a dogged logic about his north-country mind that insisted on putting first things first, and to him the first thing here was to get her away from this incessant persecution.

The bright shine of happiness in her eyes deceived him. 'You'll do it, won't you, Tina? You'll come away and start a new life?'

For a moment he did not understand as she shook her head. 'I can't, Michael. It's quite impossible.' Then she threw herself against him, burying her face so that her voice was muffled. 'But thank you for asking me. I wanted to hear that so much.'

He had to grit his teeth to keep his emotion

back as he gazed down at her bright, bowed head. 'Why is it so impossible? Tell me.'

'I have told you. Without my salary my family would be homeless. And if I left Sabastian might take his revenge on them.'

He gave a sudden vicious growl. 'I'll go and see him. It's the only way. I ought to have done it before.'

Her head jerked up in alarm. 'No! What good would it do me if you got hurt? Do you hear me, Michael? You mustn't even think of doing such a thing!'

His angry eyes stared at her. 'What difference does it make to your family if you stay or not – he's still putting the pressure on. And he'll put it on harder and harder the longer you hold out. So in the long run where's the difference whether you go or stay?'

'I can't go. I can't desert them now after having got them into this trouble.'

'But you didn't get them into it. It's not your fault the sadistic devil takes it out of them too.'

Her voice drooped wearily. 'My fault or not – does it make any difference? They're still paying for my stubbornness.'

He muttered a curse and seized her arms, bruising the flesh. 'Did you hear that? – stubbornness, you called it. That's what's going to happen – you'll go on blaming yourself more and more until you marry him believing it's the only right thing to do. You might even end up by being grateful to him when he takes the pressure off afterwards... You must get out, Tina – before it's too late.'

There was a frantic urgency in the way she pulled back and pushed his arms away. 'No, Michael. It's no use – I can't go. Please don't talk any more about it.'

She would not look at him and he realised too much tension and resistance had been built up for his plea to have any hope of success tonight. With her arms around her knees she stared out across the bay. The sun, now red and low on the horizon, gave her skin the brown flush of a briar rose and brought a red-gold glow to her hair. He felt an ache as he watched her and was jealous of each wasted second. To regain her attention he said the first thing that came into his mind.

'I went to the Grotto this afternoon.'

Her own anxiety to end the silence showed in the instant turn of her head. 'Did you? Over the cliffs?'

'Yes. I found the path you told us about and went down to have a look inside.'

A ripple of alarm showed in her eyes. 'You shouldn't have done that. It's supposed to be very dangerous.'

'I thought you didn't believe all this talk about it being haunted.'

Her voice was hesitant. 'I don't know about that. But I do think it is dangerous.'

'But not for little girls with pig-tails,' he grinned. 'If you could go there twice when you were small I ought to be allowed there now I'm big.'

Lovers are like children: their laugher is as close as their tears. She laughed, he reached out for her, and for a long moment there was nothing more in the world than happiness and one another. Then he felt her start and saw her eyes were staring over his arm at the cliff. He listened – and heard the shrill voices and distant laughter of children.

Cristina was already on her feet, her terrified eyes seeking a hiding place. Michael tried to calm her. 'They can't see us. There's nothing to get alarmed about.'

They listened, as tensed as hunted stags. For a moment there was no other sound than the rustle of the wave-swept pebbles behind them. Then came a fresh outburst of chatter and laughter that seemed to move from left to right, and Michael realised that the children were riding bicycles along the cliff path. The sound died again, and for a full thirty seconds they heard nothing. Michael was just turning to comfort Cristina when he heard the distant rustle of bushes...

Her tensed-up fear exploded. 'They're coming down... Oh, *Santissima Madonna*: they mustn't see you. We must hide somewhere...'

She dragged him behind the ridge of

boulders on which they had been sitting. The boulders were high enough to give cover if they lay flat behind them, but useless if the visitants walked down the beach. Behind the rocks was a narrow channel of sand and then the bushes of the cove's northern pro-montory. The bush roots were thick, but they found a narrow gap between them and forced their way in. They found a small patch of sand behind a broad-leaved bush and huddled down. They were no more than a yard from the channel of sand outside, on a slightly higher level than the boulders which were another five yards away. Through the branches of the bush they peered across the cove, tensely watching the point where the path led out on the beach.

Cristina was shivering as though chilled to the bone. Something of her fear communi-cated itself to Michael: his throat felt dry and his stomach tight. He put an arm round her and his lips to her cheek. 'Don't worry,' he whispered. 'We should be safe enough in here.'

She made a brave attempt to smile but her face was stiff and pale. They heard the shrill voices again, louder now, and a few seconds later three girls ran out of the bushes.

They were girls in early adolescence, two of them wearing short-length black slacks and bright blouses, the third wearing a blue frock. The girl in the frock was carrying a straw bag which she dropped near the bushes. They kicked off their sandals and then, leggy in their youth, chased one another to the water's edge Michael glanced at Cristina.

'Do you know any of them?' he whispered.

She nodded jerkily. 'Yes; they're all from Veronia. I don't know all their names but one is the daughter of Perez, a storeman who works for Sabastian.'

The girls had sampled the water by this time, found it to their liking, and were now discarding their clothes over by the bushes. One of them was making a great deal of fuss over it, giggling as she removed each garment. A minute later they were chasing one another across the beach again. They wore no costumes, and their half-formed breasts jerked in the red-orange sunlight as they plunged into the waves.

Michael glanced at Cristina. 'It doesn't look as if it's the first time they've used this place.'

Her expression was a mixture of embarrassment, fear and perplexity. 'I thought the same as Pietro: that no one would come as far as this in the evenings to swim. Most of the young people use a beach north of Veronia.'

The girls played around in the water for over ten minutes, their leaping bodies brown among the white waves. Then one of them ran back across the sand to the straw bag. She pulled out a ball, shouted at one of the girls in the sea and threw the ball at her. In a moment the three of them had formed a triangle on the beach and were throwing the ball to one another.

The girl nearest Cristina and Michael, the daughter of Perez, was a pretty child with an elfin face and black hair that the seawater had curled into ringlets. At first she stood near the water's edge, but after she had missed the ball a few times and had to run among the waves to retrieve it she began moving further back until she was standing in front of the ridge of boulders. The ball kept striking the rocks, and under his protecting arm Michael could feel Cristina's body tightening like a wound spring. Once the ball bounced over the rocks and fell into the channel of sand behind them. The elfin-faced girl ran round the rocks, her slim, brown body a thing of beauty in the evening sunlight. To Michael's relief she saw the ball immediately, snatched it up and ran back, her feet throwing up tiny spurts of golden sand. For a moment the tension eased. Then the ball flew over the rocks again and this time dropped with a shower of sand at the foot of a bush only a few feet from Michael. Cristina's eyes were huge pools of fear as she stared at it.

The girl ran around the rocks again. For a moment her eyes were occupied searching the sand, and setting his teeth Michael stretched out an arm. He had to use infinite care; the leaves were dry and rustled as his hand crept through them. He dared not shift his body for fear of shaking the bush and yet, although he stretched his fingertips to their agonised limit, he was still a few inches short of the ball. He was about to take a chance and push himself forward when the young girl turned and came up the channel of sand. There was no time to withdraw his arm. Leaving it outstretched he froze down again in the sand.

Lying awkwardly as he was, with his head half-turned, he could see the girl clearly through the matted twigs of the bush. She was close enough for every detail to register on his tensed mind: the perplexity in her frowning, childlike eyes, a mole on her left shoulder, the patches of sand that clung to her naked body. One of her companions shouted something from behind the rocks. The girl answered in a shrill impatient voice. 'The ball's gone into the bushes. I'm looking for it.'

Her hands, gloved in sand, swept aside the very twigs of the bush in front of them. Michael felt the slow, uncontrolled trembling of Cristina and damned the ill luck that brought the girls to the cove that evening. Fascinated his eyes watched the frowning girl, expecting her friends to join in the search at any moment. She moved a few feet to the right of them, directly opposite the ball. Once more she went down on her knees and swept back the twigs with her hands. This time she gave a low cry of satisfaction. Protecting her face from the branches with one arm she leaned forward to pick up the ball. And then she saw Michael's arm, lying in the sand two feet from it.

For a moment she was like a young deer that had stepped on a boa-constrictor, too paralysed with the horror of it to move a muscle. Then her eyes jerked round and saw Michael and Cristina. Recognition mixed with the blaze of fear in them before she let out a scream and leapt back. Another scream and she ran round the rocks. Almost dully Michael heard her hysterical voice calling to the other girls and their answering screams as they ran for their clothes.

Cristina was chalk white to the lips as he helped her sit upright. 'That was Perez's daughter. Did she recognise us? Could you tell?'

He nodded heavily. 'I'm afraid she did. She certainly saw both of us.'

'Then we mustn't waste a second. They'll tell everyone in Veronia as soon as they get back.'

He realised she was probably right: the girls' nakedness on the beach would add a piquancy to their story. A sudden ugly anger welled up inside him as he pushed a way through the bushes and held them back for

Cristina to follow him. She glanced across the beach.

'They've gone already... Hurry, Michael. If they're riding bicycles they can be in Veronia in a quarter of an hour.'

His stubbornness to threats made his voice rebellious. 'Why should we go at all? We're free people; we're doing no wrong here.'

She stared at him. 'Don't you understand what will happen? Sabastian will send his men out immediately. You'll be in terrible danger...'

'To hell with Sabastian.' His face was as black and savage as a thunder-cloud. 'I don't want to go.'

'You must go. For my sake... How will I feel if you are attacked and injured...?'

His blind anger resented her fear. 'If we run every time people see us together we may as well give up the fight. I thought you wanted to defy him.'

'You know the reason I'm afraid, Michael. Surely you must know that...' Then, as that reason overwhelmed everything else, her pleading became panic-stricken. 'The time we are wasting here arguing like this... Holy Mother, have you gone crazy? They'll move like lightning once they hear. You can't fight half a dozen men.'

The knowledge she was right did nothing to dispel his anger. He followed her sullenly across the sand and into the bushes, tearing their swinging branches aside as savagely as if they were the arms of men trying to prevent him following her.

They could see nothing of the three girls when they reached the cliff top. The sun had set and the sea below was dark green and rose in the twilight. Sobbing for breath Cristina hurried him along the path. At the point where the road looped out from the hills she hesitated a moment before pointing to the valley.

'Perhaps it might be safer to go that way... Yes ... I think it may be. Please hurry, Michael. The girls will have reached Veronia ten minutes ago.'

He turned up the dirt road without comment, his sullen anger following on his heels like a huge black dog. They followed the road around the hill. As the hill rose between them and the sunset the twilight deepened. It was deathly quiet except for the scuffle of their feet and Cristina's sobbing breathing. In a field on their left trusses of hay bound around upright poles looked like African huts in the fading light. A bullock cart appeared from nowhere. The driver, an old man, called out a greeting to them as he passed by and then the road was empty again. Five minutes more and Michael put an abrupt hand on Cristina's arm.

'You can't keep this pace up all the way to town. Take it a little easier.'

She had to fight for breath to answer him. 'We've no time to waste … they're sure to have heard by this time. I think we ought to separate soon. It might be safer for you.'

They both heard the sound of the approaching engine at the same time. Cristina stiffened and threw a frantic glance at the vineyards alongside the road. But there was no time to take even the scanty cover they offered – a hill shoulder had held back the noise of the engine until it was too late. The lorry came round the corner at speed and pulled up in front of them with a squeal of brakes. Four men jumped down from it, and before Cristina could break her paralysis and cry a warning to Michael they were surrounded.

CHAPTER 13

Three of the men Cristina recognised as labourers who worked in Sabastian's store. The fourth, blue-chinned and cloth-capped, was Perez, the father of the girl who had discovered them. He was carrying a heavy stick and there was a look of satisfaction on his coarse face.

Cristina heard her voice, distant with fear and reproach. 'You should have run... They wouldn't dare harm me. You might have got away…'

Michael's face was pale but tight-set as he stared round the ring of men. Perez, thick voice harsh, took a step nearer him. 'My daughter says you were spying on her down on the beach. Her and her two friends, while they were swimming!'

His heavy island accent caused Michael some difficulty and Cristina answered quickly for him. 'He hasn't been spying on anybody. He has been with me all the evening.'

Perez turned and shouted. To Cristina's dismay a slight figure jumped down from the cab of the lorry and advanced towards them. It was the young, elfin-faced girl, now pale and demure in her blue frock. Perez pointed at Michael. 'Was this the man you saw watching you from the bushes?'

She nodded, avoiding Michael's eyes. Perez grunted his satisfaction, ordered her back into the lorry, and then turned to Cristina.

'This is the man she saw all right. He was hiding in the bushes, the filthy foreigner, watching them get undressed. We've come to teach him a lesson.'

She was ashen with fear for him. 'I tell you he wasn't watching them. He was with me. He's been with me the whole evening.'

'Why should my daughter lie? She saw him in the bushes. What was he doing there?'

164

She suddenly saw the trap they were in. But there was a hundred-to-one chance Perez had come of his own accord and for that reason alone she had to answer the question.

'He was with me. We did not want to be seen...'

Her face burned at the suggestive glances of the other three men. Perez shared their amusement only for a moment; his brutal face was threatening again as he turned back to her. 'Perhaps the Englishman did take you into the bushes, perhaps you arranged to go with him – I don't know about that. But I do know that he watched my daughter and her friends undress, and for that he is a filthy pig who deserves the thrashing he is going to get.'

There was a frightening genuineness about his anger as his thick hands gripped the heavy stick. Frantic with fear she ran in front of Michael. 'You can't blame him if your daughter isn't decent enough to wear a bathing suit. She's the one at fault, not he.'

Perez was working himself up into the blind fury of the peasant. 'The filthy foreigner didn't have to watch her. If he'd shown himself they would all have run away. Get out of my way, Cristina Delfano.'

One of the other three men caught hold of her arm and dragged her aside. Michael, who had been standing as motionless as a threatened bulldog during the last two minutes, cursed and hit the man with all his strength. He gave a groan and dropped on the road. It was the signal for the other three men to attack, Perez leading them. He gave a growl of fury as Cristina caught hold of his stick and tore it from her, almost throwing her to the ground. As she tried to run after him the man lying on the road recovered and seized her ankle. She struggled to free herself but he pulled himself upright and tried to smother her arms. Half-mad with fear for Michael she fought like a wildcat, scratching at his face with her nails. Behind her she heard the thud of blows and the gasps of struggling men.

She did not hear the approach of the convertible car until it pulled up in a swirl of dust a few yards away. The singular fortuitousness of its arrival escaped her at that moment; she was conscious only of relief as the three men attacking Michael turned sharply to face it. He, with blood running down his face and his coat half-torn from his back, tore himself away and turned with a growl to help her. The man holding her released his grip hurriedly and she ran towards him.

'Are you all right, Michael...? Are you badly hurt?'

He shook his head, his raging eyes on the low-slung car and its owner. Sabastian, a debonair figure in a black blouse and silk scarf, jumped out and called a sharp order to the four men. They moved towards him and he drew Perez aside, talking to him in a low voice. For a moment they seemed to be arguing: Perez's face was sullen. Then Perez nodded his head grudgingly and waved the other three men over to him. Sabastian spoke to them all and then approached Michael and Cristina. Although his voice was quiet there was an undertone of anger in it as he motioned to his car.

'I think you had both better come back to town with me. Quickly, if you please.'

Michael's bleeding face was black with suspicion. 'What's your game, Cerone?'

Twilight hid the Italian's expression. 'My game, as you call it, is to get you safely away from these men. As you've already found out they're very angry with you.' His resentful gaze moved to Cristina. 'But stay here if you wish, of course.'

She had no hesitation, pulling at Michael's arm. 'Don't argue. Get in the car – quickly.'

To reach the car they had to pass by the group of sullen men. Cristina tried to walk between them and Michael. He pulled her angrily to his opposite side. In the car Cristina took one of the rear seats. Sabastian's lips thinned as he saw her choice, but he made no comment when Michael took the seat alongside him. He started the engine and swung the car round on the road. A moment later they were heading for Veronia, the four men and the lorry vanishing behind them in the twilight.

None of them spoke a word on the way to Veronia. Outside the hotel Sabastian switched off the engine and turned to Michael.

'Now, signor; I want to give you a little advice. Until your boat sails on Thursday I should stay very near to your hotel. You have seen how angry the islanders are at what happened tonight – if you are not careful you may be attacked again and I can't always guarantee to be near enough to help you.'

Michael's mood of aggression, brought out by the fight, was still at flash point. 'What are you getting at – what happened tonight?'

Mockery was a will o' the wisp in Sabastian's voice. 'In small towns one cannot help hearing things – if I had not heard I would not have been able to rescue you. The men believe you were hiding in a clump of bushes watching three girls undress. And the girls all swear it is true.'

'It's a lie. You know damned well it wasn't the reason I was there.'

'The reason I believe may be different' – here Sabastian could not hide his aversion of the Englishman – 'I am telling you what others believe and how you can remain safe from them until Thursday.'

Michael jumped from the car. 'Thanks for nothing. What other people's dirty minds think isn't going to change my ways one jot. Nor their threats' – and his scowling eyes challenged Sabastian – 'or anyone else's.'

He opened the door for Cristina to jump out. She hesitated, then shook her head. 'I'd like to have a word with Sabastian first, Michael. You go inside and have those cuts attended to.'

The scowl on his bruised face grew. As her eyes begged him to understand he gave a curt nod. 'All right. I'll phone you in half an hour.' With that he turned and tramped up the verandah steps to the hotel.

Sabastian gave a contemptuous laugh. 'So polite, your English friend. So grateful for being saved from a beating up.'

'Do you expect us to be grateful? Do you believe we don't suspect you?'

He seemed less surprised at her suspicions than bitter at the inevitability of them.

'Suspect, *cara*. What do you mean by that?'

'Surely you don't think you've deceived me. I recognised the lorry, Sabastian, as well as the men... When you heard what had happened you saw how you could use it to advantage and went straight to Perez. You worked on his temper – told him that a man who lies in bushes staring at young girls

169

ought to get a lesson – and when he was in the right frame of mind you lent him a lorry and three men to go with it.'

'And then I went out to rescue your English friend from the trap that I'd laid. Is that what you're saying?'

'Yes,' she said fiercely. 'You saw a way of killing two birds with one stone: of getting Michael into trouble and then coming like a knight in shining armour to his rescue. But you didn't have time to do it properly – you had to send three of your workmen and one of your own lorries. Who did you send along the cliff path – Mario and his cronies?'

Her lips curled at his show of controlled resentment.

'I can't win, can I, *cara mia*. If I put men on your boy friends I am a bully; if I save them from a beating I am a cheat. As a cheat is no better than a bully I may as well sit back in the future and let things take their course.'

This threat to Michael took much of the sting from her anger. 'Why can't you leave him alone? He has done you no harm and he's leaving on Thursday.'

'Done me no harm…' At this the young Italian's resentment spilled over. 'He has taken you to a café where everyone in town could see you alone together. He has let everyone see his interest in you. And tonight he persuaded you to see him alone in the cove…'

'Why shouldn't I see him if I am willing? What right does that give you to threaten him with violence.'

'He is a foreigner. He is here for only a few days, enjoying himself. Why should I allow him to make love to you?'

The balcony of Michael's bedroom was close by and she was afraid he might overhear. Knowing Sabastian would follow her she jumped from the car. 'What about Emilio and Vittorio – were they foreigners too?' She turned away bitterly. 'But what's the use of talking to you. I'm going home now.'

He followed her along the pavement and caught hold of her arm. '*Cara mia,* don't be angry with me until you've listened to what I have to say. At least I did not let Michael come to any harm tonight.'

His words made her pause. The piazza was in deep twilight, the tables around the hotel verandah empty as yet. Beyond the jetty a faint yellow afterglow separated sea and sky. She listened to his changed voice.

'I'm a man, *cara,* and I know more about men than you. This is only a holiday romance for him. Once he is back in England with his family and his friends it will just be another pleasant memory. It can't be anything else, with his only knowing you a few days. But you and I are different, *cara.* We have known one another all our lives.'

Sincerity purged all intimidation and

mockery from him. For the moment he looked as she remembered him as a youth, clean-faced, upright, tremblingly alive.

'I've known you since you were a little girl, *cara*. And I've never sopped loving you, not for a day, not for an hour. I know I've done some bad things to you, but I've done them because I want you so much. I told you once that you had the power to lift me to heaven or drop me to hell, and you laughed and said I was being melodramatic. But it's true, *cara*. When I see you with other men – even though I know they are nothing but friends – I still go mad with jealousy. Marry me, Tina, and I'll be a different man. I swear it – I swear it on the Holy Mother.'

Seeing she was listening he drew nearer to her. 'I'll make you the happiest girl on the island, *cara*. There'll be nothing you can't have. Think of the friends we used to be, *cara*. Surely it must still mean something to you.'

Her voice was low and sad. 'Of course it still means something. Do you think I haven't cried my eyes out seeing how money and power have changed you? It's the power I'm afraid of, Sabastian. It has hold of you by the throat and it's choking all the decency out of you. And I'm afraid that nothing in the world can drag you away from it now.'

Before she could move he caught hold of her hands. He was laughing with exultation. 'Do you realise what you've just said, *cara?*

You still care what happens to me! That means you still love me. Marry me, Tina. Say yes and we'll set the town alight with our happiness. And tomorrow your father will have his shop flooded with orders.'

His mention of her father was a mistake. She remembered Pietro's words and all her resistance was back as she pulled her hands sharply from him. 'No, Sabastian. It's too late. You've broken him now, just as you've broken all those other people. They've lost all faith and confidence in themselves – you can't give that back.' She wanted to add: 'Nor can you give us back the wonderful childhood faith we had in them,' but the words choked in her throat.

He saw she was escaping and his voice lunged out to hold her. 'It's not too late, *cara*. If you marry me everything will be just as it was. I swear it on the Holy Mother.'

She turned back to him. 'You'll give the broken old men their spirits back? You'll bring back their children who had to leave the island when there was no food…? You'll make them forget all their bitterness? You'll be God and change the past? That's what you're saying, Sabastian.'

'I only did those things because I love you, *cara*. Can't you see that?'

'Not all of them, Sabastian. Not all.'

In the darkness his face was turning sullen again. 'You've never been the same since you went to England. It made you into a snob. We're not good enough for you now – you'd rather go out with a foreigner than with someone you've known all your life.'

The remark stung her to anger. 'How can you say such things – when you yourself have prevented my going out with my friends.'

'What friend have you got who has known you longer or would do as much for you as I?'

The strain of the evening had left her with a feeling of weary hopelessness. 'I know you care for me. And I still like you – when you're not being vindictive. But I can't marry you, Sabastian. However I tried I wouldn't be able to forget the things you've done. And so it wouldn't be fair to either of us.'

For a moment his black eyes glowed their appeal again. 'Try it, *carissima*. Try it for the sake of our childhood days.'

'No, Sabastian. It wouldn't work. Please believe me it wouldn't and don't ask me again.'

Because of the past she had tried to make her refusal as gentle as possible. She also wanted to use the rare moment of forbearance to plead for her family. But as her eyes lifted to his face the idea snapped in her mind like a broken thread. His dark, twisted expression told her the devil in him was in command again.

'What about the Englishman? Are you going to try to see him again?'

She could not hide her sadness. 'Why do you bother so much about him? He is leaving on Thursday.'

'No foreigner is going to make a holiday plaything out of you, no matter how long he stays. He isn't going to take you into the bushes again and shame you before the whole island.'

The change in him was so vicious it frightened rather than angered her. 'You know the reason we had to hide there. If you would leave us alone here in town we wouldn't have to go around the island like criminals.'

The black emanation of his jealousy poisoned the air around them. His voice had a fine tremor, like a cruel, vibrating blade. 'If you care about him at all, *cara mia,* keep away from him until Thursday when his ship sails. Keep away, I say. For if I cannot have you, then no one else shall. That I promise you.'

'There's a devil in you, Sabastian,' she breathed. 'If you don't conquer it, it will destroy you.'

His voice mocked her. 'Mind it doesn't destroy others first. Remember what I have told you.'

He was a stranger standing before her, cruel of face and without pity. She stared at him a moment, then turned and ran sobbing down the pavement towards the shop.

Michael came down from his bedroom and

walked across the hall to the telephone. As he lifted the receiver from its hook he noticed the pale-faced youth at the desk eyeing his bruised face with curiosity. The island had no automatic exchange and he had to juggle with the hook for a full minute before the operator replied. He gave the number of Delfano's shop and waited anxiously.

A woman's voice addressed him. It was mature in tone and he guessed it belonged to Maria, Cristina's stepmother.

'Yes. Who is that?'

'May I speak to Signorina Delfano, please?'

The woman's voice came back, suspicious and probing. 'Who is that speaking?'

'My name is Forbes. Michael Forbes.'

The woman had heard of the night's happenings: he could tell it by the sudden edge to her voice. 'What do you want, signor?'

'I want to speak to Signorina Delfano. Will you please call her for me?'

Maria made no pains to conceal her dislike. 'Wait a moment. I'll see if she is here.'

Michael gazed round the hall. Through the open door of the lounge the lazy movement of the ceiling fan caught his eyes, barely stirring the sultry evening air. Three linen-suited men sat at a table near the window, chatting over a bottle of wine. He did not know them and they seemed to have no interest in him. He shifted his position, rubbing a tender spot on his shoulder where Perez's stick had landed. He heard a movement at the other end of the line, followed by Cristina's low voice.

'Hello. Is that you, Michael?'

'Yes. I waited until the car had gone before I phoned.' He paused, frowned. 'You were a long time talking to him. What happened?'

He could feel her restraint and guessed she believed her stepmother was listening. 'We argued for a while. About the usual things…'

'Had he organised that party tonight? Did you find out?'

'Yes. He as good as admitted it. Not that I hadn't guessed.'

The bruises became livid on his scowling face. 'I was a fool. I ought to have dragged him from the car and given him a good hiding.' He shifted from one foot to the other, as restless as a baited bulldog. 'When am I going to see you again? Will you come round and have a drink with me now? It's only nine-thirty.'

For a moment there was no sound and he thought she had not heard him. When she spoke her voice was so low she seemed to have withdrawn halfway across the world.

'Michael; you must listen to me. We have to stop seeing one another. If we don't something is going to happen to you and I could not bear it.'

The muscles of his hand clenching the receiver bunched into hard ridges. 'No. We're not giving in – especially after what happened tonight. Come round and see me now. He can't do very much in here.'

'No, Michael; I've made up my mind. You might have been seriously hurt tonight; the next time you will be. Stay near the hotel until Thursday and then catch the ship and forget about me. It is better that way for both of us.'

'I'm going to see you again,' he said doggedly. 'Help me to arrange a meeting.'

'But I don't want us to meet. It can only make matters worse because I can't go away with you. And if you were hurt as well it would be terrible. Can't you see that?'

He could see nothing but his need to be with her. But her concern for his safety made her equally resolute. 'I'll see you off on the ship on Thursday,' was the only promise he could wring from her. 'I'll be on the jetty without fail.'

In his frustration he did not know what angry words he used, but he heard her crying as he hung up the receiver. His temper was ugly, and the sight of the pale-faced youth staring at him curiously made his fists clench. Somehow he found himself back in his room again, alone in the darkness of his mood.

CHAPTER 14

Michael slept badly that night and awoke early. His first thought was that he would force a meeting on Cristina, but freed of his temper of the previous night he realised that a meeting for its own sake could only exacerbate the existing problem. At the best it would only make his departure on the following day more painful; at the worst it might mean physical injury to him. To make such risks worthwhile he had to offer her entirely new suggestions on the solving of her problem. She had already refused his offer to pay her passage to the mainland. What alternatives, then, were left?

The only one he could think of was marriage. And this brought forth all his north-country caution that stood like an immobile fell behind the quickly-roused, often blinding, mist of his temper. It was not that he had any doubts about his affection for Cristina – if this was not love he would never know its meaning. But although two years in the Army out East had liberated him from most of the inhibitions of an English middle-class upbringing, its implanted views on marriage had not been touched. A man and a girl ought to become engaged first... Parents ought to be consulted and given a chance to meet one another... And most of all a man ought to have a home to offer his wife, to have money or at least the security of employment ... and he would almost certainly have none of these things if he stayed on to marry her.

He hated his caution and reviled it, but it sat in his mind as unperturbed as a wise old sage, reminding him of yet another problem. It was true that Sabastian could hardly continue his direct persecution of Cristina if she became his wife, but it gave no guarantee that he would not take his revenge on her family. And with that fear in her mind, would she leave them. And if she would not, what hope was there for him to find work on an impoverished Mediterranean island where Sabastian held all the keys of influence in his hand?

As it stood there seemed no single answer to the problem. What he needed most of all was time – time to have long intimate talks with her so that he could find out every relevant detail before making a decision. As he paced restlessly up and down his bedroom he found himself glancing repeatedly at his watch, morbidly watching the rapid passing of the minutes.

His fretting was not helped by the weather. On his awakening the sky had been cloudy for the first time since his arrival, and although it had cleared now the sultriness of the heat gave warning that rain was on its way.

He could not count the times he decided to meet her at the lunch hour, only to change his mind. His indecision was not due to fear of physical danger; by this time his fretting mind was in a state almost to welcome it as a distraction. It was the pathetic undertone he had caught in her voice the previous evening. 'I love you, Michael, and I would gladly give half my life to go away with you on Thursday. But because I cannot, don't make it worse for me. Please don't do that, Michael.'

He felt the sweat in his clenched hands. He paced the bedroom again and then shook his head. It was like a prison echoing his tortured thoughts back from its four walls. He had to escape from it; perhaps outside, under the sky, it might be easier to make a decision.

He went downstairs and out on the verandah. Across the piazza the morning market was in full swing: small groups of women peering at the fish on the stalls, their chatter mingling with the shrill cries of the fishwives. As he stood there Michael suddenly remembered Pietro, a friend, someone he could trust… A sudden eagerness to talk to the old man made him run down the steps. Out in the piazza the sun was fierce, burning through his thin nylon shirt. As he passed the fish stalls he was conscious of the stares of the women and their avid whispering. One of them called something out to him in a shrill, derisive voice. He guessed its meaning a moment later when a cackle of laughter and jeering followed it. He walked grimly on towards the jetty, his neck burning with embarrassment and anger.

The jetty was quiet: the fishing fleet had been out all night and the crews were sleeping. Michael walked the full length of it but could see nothing of Pietro. On the harbour side a boat, with two huge lamps fitted fore and aft to attract fish, nosed against the bottom of a flight of steps. Two men, stripped to the waist, appeared to be working on the electrical equipment. Recognising neither of them Michael went halfway down the steps and gave them a call.

'Do either of you know where Pietro is this morning?'

They turned and gazed up at him with curiosity. One was shock-haired and swarthy, with a pair of small, humorous eyes. He grinned up at Michael. 'The island is full of Pietros, signor. But there is only one with a big laugh. Is that the one you mean?'

'That's the one. Do you know where he is?'

'No, signor. He hasn't been down this morning.'

'Where else could he be? Do you know?'

The man looked at his companion who shrugged his shoulders. 'We don't know, signor. He is usually here in the mornings, but today he hasn't come.'

Michael had found comfort in the thought of a talk with Pietro – the old man had known Cristina since she was a child and might have had some useful advise to offer. Now he felt badly let down as he thanked the men and climbed back up the steps to the jetty.

He hesitated on reaching the piazza, dallied with the idea of taking a walk, and finally tramped red-faced and glowering past the stalls back to the hotel. It was now eleven-thirty – if he were going to see Cristina he had an hour left before she returned home from school. He went to his room, wrote two letters, and then returned restlessly to the verandah. The stalls had closed now and the piazza had emptied of people. On a sudden impulse he went over to a table in the far corner. She normally passed the hotel on her way home, and if he waited here she could not fail to see him.

It was a compromise, he had no love of compromises but in the situation it seemed the only choice he could make. If she changed her mind she could go into the hotel with him where they might have a chance of talking undisturbed, at least for a while. On the other hand if she remained firm to her resolution he would not try to make her break it.

Such, at least, was the promise he made himself. He sat at the table, lit a cigarette, and waited with his eyes fixed on the distant gap in the pavement where the Vicolo Giovanni ran into the piazza. Each time someone came out of the street his body stiffened. It was quiet now and he could hear the murmur of the sea. He threw away his cigarette and lit a second one.

Half a dozen children suddenly ran out of the street, their shrill laughter scattering a cluster of dozing pigeons. A woman followed them, carrying a huge basket full of washing. A few more children ran out and then there was a lull. From somewhere along the waterfront the dull rumble of a crane bruised the hot noon air.

By the time Michael had finished a third cigarette he knew she was not coming. She had either stayed on at school or he had missed her. He stepped down into the piazza and realised she could have come down one of the streets further along it and so avoided passing the hotel.

As he stood there he suddenly knew that he must see her – that all the risks, even the risks to herself, had to be taken unless they were both to spend the rest of their lives in vain regret. Turning sharply away from his doubts and fears, not allowing himself another moment's hesitation, he started towards the shop.

He was conscious of his quickened heart-beats as he pushed open the shop door. The sun-blinds were down, and after the brilliant sunlight outside the shop seemed almost dark. Then his eyes adjusted themselves and he gazed curiously at the pieces of boat gear and hardware as he walked to the counter at the far end.

Summoned by the tinkle of the bell Carlo Delfano shuffled into the shop, a dejected figure in his old black suit. On seeing Michael he paused, a look of apprehension coming into his eyes. Then he approached the counter slowly.

'*Buona sera, signor.*'

Michael had not missed Carlo's hesitation. He knew ... probably everything. But then he would – Sabastian would have seen to that. He began cautiously.

'*Buona sera, signor.* Are you Signor Delfano?'

In spite of his anxiety there was a certain old-world courtesy and dignity about Carlo. 'I am, signor. What may I do for you?'

'I'd very much like a word with your daughter, Cristina, signor, if you would be so kind as to call her. My name is Michael Forbes.'

The apprehension spread in Carlo's

melancholy eyes. He threw an uneasy glance at the half-open door behind him before answering Michael in a low voice.

'She has not come back from the school yet, signor. Is there anything I can do for you?'

He seemed about to continue and then paused, as though leaving the onus of the next move on his visitor. His behaviour puzzled Michael, who, particularly after Maria's curtness on the telephone the previous evening, had supposed both parents resented his efforts to persuade Cristina to leave the island. Yet in this sad-faced man's eyes he could almost imagine seeing a mute plea for understanding. It surprised him and gave his voice more confidence.

'It is important I see her today. Have you any idea when she will be back?'

Carlo's voice was so low as to be almost inaudible. 'She is usually home at least half an hour before this, signor. But perhaps some of the children have been misbehaving and she is keeping them in...'

His voice trailed off and Michael saw that a tall, raven-haired woman had appeared in the rear doorway. He recognised animosity at once in her black eyes as they fixed on him. Then she swung them on Carlo, her voice curt. 'What are you doing? Your lunch is getting cold.'

Carlo made a gallant although abortive

effort to cover the reason for Michael's presence. 'I am just attending to this gentleman, Mamma. I will be with you in a moment.'

Maria did not move, and Michael saw from the aggressive line of her black eyebrows that she had overheard everything. She turned back to him.

'Was it you who phoned and spoke to Cristina last night?'

He nodded.

'What is it you want now? To speak to her again?'

'Yes,' he said quietly. 'I'd be very grateful if you'd ask her to phone me at the hotel as soon as she gets back.'

Her bold, challenging eyes travelled up and down him. 'What is it you want with her? I would like to know.'

The bluntness of the question made Michael flush. Carlo, shocked, made a brave protest. 'Mamma, you have no right to ask such a question. Cristina is not a child – we must give her the gentleman's message.'

Maria had the fuse of her temper already primed. All she needed was a spark, and this was it. *'Santa Maria;* what kind of a man are you? Don't you care anything about the reputation of your daughter?'

'Mamma, you must not say such things. The signor is a gentleman – he means no harm to Tina.'

Her hands leapt to her hips. 'Does he not,

indeed? Then what is all the talk that has been going around the town last night and this morning?'

'But, Mamma, we know the reason for it. All decent people know the reason...'

She gave him no chance to finish. 'The reason, indeed. What stories will the girl tell us next?' She swung round on Michael. 'Signor, you must leave our daughter alone. You have brought scandal on her and I will have no more of it.'

Michael's face was pale with dismay and anger. 'If you'll give me a chance I can explain everything that happened last night.'

Her lips curled. 'We have heard the story once from Cristina – we do not want to hear it again.'

'But it's quite true. The cove was the only place where we could go to escape from Cerone's men. Surely I haven't to remind you what he is doing to her.'

'And you, of course, are improving matters with your interference?'

He saw the futility of argument and turned appealingly to Carlo. 'Will you give her my message, signor? That is all I ask.'

Maria's voice leapt at him before Carlo could reply. 'No, he will not. The girl has got herself into enough trouble because of you already. Besides' – and Maria's hard eyes were triumphant – 'she does not wish to see you again. I heard her tell you so last night.

Is that not enough for you?'

Again Michael ignored her. 'Your daughter and I have become good friends, Signor Delfano, and I want to help her all I can. Please give her my message.'

His resistance exploded the last of Maria's restraint. Some of her rapid words were unintelligible to him, others struck him like whips. 'Get out of this shop and don't come back... And keep away from the girl or you'll be sorry you ever set foot on this island. We don't like your sort in these parts...'

Temper racked him but somehow he fought it back. Enough trouble had been caused already, and Cristina would pay for it as dearly as her father. He allowed Carlo to hurry him to the door.

'I'm sorry about this, Signor Delfano. But it is very important I see her: my boat sails tomorrow.'

Carlo, with his back to Maria, grimaced a mute message as he half-pushed Michael into the street. 'I understand, signor. But it is better you go now. *Arrivederci.*'

The shop door was hastily shut in Michael's face. From behind it he heard the shrillness of Maria's voice. His thoughts defied description as he started back for the hotel.

He had almost reached the verandah steps when he saw Cristina. She was crossing the piazza from the northern waterfront, stumbling over the cobblestones as if she were blind. He ran towards her and saw she was crying. She saw him, gave a moan of relief and threw herself into his arms.

'Oh, Michael. Michael…'

His voice was harsh, alarmed. 'What is it, darling?'

She tried to speak but a paroxysm of grief choked her. Her hands gripped him in agony, dug into his arms. Frightened he pulled back her head.

'What's happened. Tell me.'

She shook her head free and buried her face again in his shoulder. Through his thin shirt he felt the scalding heat of her tears.

'I love him so much, Michael. So very much…'

He had never seen such grief. Her whole body was shuddering with it.

'Love who? What has happened? For God's sake tell me.'

Her fingers dug deeper into his arms. 'It's Pietro, Michael… They've hurt him. He's in hospital and they think he will die…'

For a moment the sunlit piazza swam before his eyes. 'They've hurt Pietro? But why? What did he do?'

'It happened this morning, when the fishing fleet got back. Pietro must have heard what happened last night and he attacked Sabastian. You know what a temper he has –

they say he drew a knife...'

Over her stricken bowed head his face was as grim as granite. 'And then?'

'Someone – I think it was Guido – pushed him away. He slipped and fell down the stone steps... They had plenty of witnesses ... they always do have ... and they all say it was Pietro's fault, so the police have taken no action. But it wasn't an accident...' Her face lifted to his in tortured protest. 'It wouldn't have happened, would it, but for all the things that Sabastian has done...?'

He shook his head slowly. His eyes turned towards the northern waterfront, and the wider range of his vision coned down to one focal point – the building where Sabastian had a store and his offices. Motionless he listened to her.

'I only heard about it an hour ago and went straight to the hospital. He was still unconscious and looked so grey and broken...' Her agony returned. 'Oh, Michael, why did it have to be him? I loved him so – he was the only friend I had...'

He put her gently aside and started walking across the piazza. Behind him there was a sudden silence, then a frightened cry. 'Michael. Where are you going?'

He had only one thought and there were no words in it. He kept on walking and men drew sharply aside at his expression.

Cristina followed him, pulling frantically

at his arm. 'No, Michael. It's playing right into his hands – he's got men in the store. And afterwards they'll all swear it was your fault, just as they swore it was Pietro's... Come back with me ... please. I can't stand any more...'

He walked on without turning his head. 'Go back to the hotel. Wait for me there.'

'It's madness to go there, Michael. You won't have a chance...'

He hardly felt her tugging at him. The building grew in his eyes until he was standing before it, a converted warehouse at the side of the narrow waterfront. She made her last bid to check him. 'Michael, if you love me, do as I ask. Come back with me to the hotel...'

He pushed his way into an office. A short counter ran from the wall on his right; behind it were two girl typists and a youth. One of the girls rose to attend him, then stepped back in alarm at his expression.

'Where's Cerone? Find him and tell him to come out here.' Then he noticed a glass-panelled door behind the desks. In a second he was round the counter and making for it.

It was half an inch ajar. He kicked it viciously, a glass panel shattering as it crashed back. He stepped inside, only to find the well-appointed office empty.

With a grunt of disappointment he turned back into the main office. Urged on by the girls, the youth tried to grab his arm. He received a push that sent him crashing backwards over a chair. Michael went up to one of the girls.

'Where's Cerone? Tell me, quickly.'

The girl pointed to a door at the opposite side of the office. Her voice was frightened. 'He went out into the warehouse some minutes ago, signor. Perhaps he has gone to lunch – I don't know.'

Michael made for the door. Cristina ran in front of him. 'You must be crazy – there'll be a dozen men in there. Come away while there's still time...'

Her voice broke off as the door opened and Sabastian, impeccable in a fawn linen suit, entered the office. His dark, handsome face showed astonishment at seeing Michael and Cristina. Seeing the square-set Englishman coming at him like a bulldog after a cat, he half-turned for the door, only to hear Michael's growl of hate. 'Scared, Cerone? Do you prefer dealing with girls and old men?'

Sabastian turned sharply back. 'Is that why you're here? Because of Pietro?'

For reply Michael smashed a fist full in his face. The Italian reeled back against the wall, recovered, and leapt forward. Michael hit him again and this time he dropped to the carpet, dazed with shock.

Cristina tugged at Michael. 'Have you

gone crazy... Run... Run while there is still time.'

Sabastian stirred, sat upright. There was a hush in the office as he struggled into a chair. His face was an ugly sight with blood pouring from his mouth. He lifted a handkerchief and dabbed at it. He seemed unable to believe what had happened as he stared first at the red stain and then at Michael.

'You come here and do this ... in front of my clerks.' He dabbed at his mouth again. '*Santa Maria,* am I dreaming this?'

Cristina, pale to the lips, was standing between them. 'He went crazy when he heard what you'd done to the old man.'

For the moment his half-stunned mind seemed to find her accusation more serious than the blows he had received from Michael. 'What I did to him...? You surely don't believe it was done deliberately?'

'Deliberately or not – what difference does it make? It still happened because of the things you've done to me. He was my friend... And now he might die.'

'*Cara;* it was an accident. He came at me with a knife. Guido pushed him away and he slipped... I'm as sorry as you about it. But it was nobody's fault.'

'Nobody's fault that he hated you! Are you telling me you don't know the reason for it?'

'I'm sorry it happened, *cara* – that's the truth. But don't blame me for it.'

'Don't blame you for it?' Michael's voice was as menacing as the growl of a bulldog that had tasted flesh and wanted more. 'You ought to be in hospital alongside the old man.'

So far contrition and shock had kept Sabastian's passion in check. Now, as his head cleared and he saw the breathless typists across the office watching them, his whole appearance and manner changed.

'You mad fool. Do you realise the position you've put yourself in – what I could do to you if I chose?'

Michael sneered his hate. 'Whatever you chose it wouldn't be to face me man to man.'

'You are calling me a coward...' For a moment there was murder in the Italian's black eyes. Then he turned to Cristina.

'In the name of the Holy Mother take this madman away. Take him away before there is another tragedy on the island.'

She could not believe her ears. 'You mean you aren't going to call your men?'

'No. There has been enough trouble for one day. But go now, in the name of all the Saints.'

She half-dragged Michael into the street. Sabastian followed them. His mouth was an ugly sight, his lips swollen and shredded. He motioned Cristina aside and against Michael's sullen protests she obeyed.

'Take the fool back to the hotel and tell him if he cares anything at all about himself, to catch the ship tomorrow. And don't try to see him again. I shall have men watching him day and night, and if you disobey me he will suffer for it.'

For a moment her defiance returned. 'What if I decide to leave the island myself? Have you thought of that?'

He nodded mockingly. 'Many times, *cara*, just as you have. And you know what I should do to those you leave behind.'

'You're a devil, not a man,' she breathed. 'I never believed I could hate anyone so much.'

His resentment spilled over like acid from an overfilled beaker. 'You've no right to hate me – not when you've put the devil in me yourself.' He lifted a shaking hand and pointed to his swollen mouth. 'I've let the Englishman strike me and I've done nothing, although in the name of self-defence I could have had him beaten to a pulp... I've done this for you and because I'm sorry for what happened to old Pietro this morning. But, by the Saints, all is over now. Let him see you once more and he'll wish he'd never been born. I give you my word on that, *cara*, and you know I never break it. If you care anything about him at all, see he catches that ship tomorrow.'

With that he swung sharply round and

went back into his office. Cristina took Michael's sullen arm and led him back to the hotel. At the foot of the verandah steps she turned to him, her voice resolute.

'I'm going home how. Don't try to see me tonight or tomorrow. Take the ship and forget all about me and this island.'

He shook his head doggedly. 'No. I must see you this evening. We must have a long talk – we can't leave things like this.'

She would not allow herself the slightest hesitation. 'What use is a talk – we've nothing new to say … it can't change anything. And another meeting will bring nothing but misery to us and perhaps to innocent people as well.' He suddenly swam in her vision as if the sea were already between them, and she knew she had only seconds left to talk.

'I mean it, Michael. I don't want to see you again. Go tomorrow and forget all about me. *Addio*, Michael. *Addio*, my darling…'

He tried to catch hold of her but she ran away. He started after her, only to realise the hopelessness of it after a few steps. As he walked slowly back his eyes fell on the cobblestones where the dark stains from her tears were already drying in the sun.

CHAPTER 15

Michael was allowed to see Pietro the following morning. The hospital, staffed by nuns, was a neat, white building at the end of the northern waterfront. As he reached the entrance he glanced back. Sabastian was keeping his word. All night two men had been stationed outside his hotel and now Mario and a fisherman were following him.

They made no pretence of concealment, Mario waving a mocking arm as he glanced back. He entered the cool hospital, trying to escape from the anger that was near destroying him.

A sweet-faced nun took him to Pietro's bed. 'We do not expect him to last long, signor; he has had the Holy Sacrament. Please try not to excite him.'

It had been his spirit that had made Pietro seem younger than his age. Now, with that spirit almost departed, his head looked like a skull on the snow white pillow. His once fierce eyes were vacant, and he showed no sign of recognition when Michael took his bony hand and talked gently to him. Yet in another dimension his spirit must have been fighting a tremendous battle with death. As the nun's eyes met Michael's and he was about to draw back, the old man's lips started moving.

At first his words were incoherent. But as Michael's grip tightened on the bony hand he could feel the grim, terrible battle the old man was fighting. He bent lower, his ear brushing Pietro's lips.

'What is it, Pietro? What are you trying to say?'

Victory came with frightening suddenness. One moment the faded blue eyes were dull, in the next they blazed with fierce life. 'Michael, lad, can you hear me? Michael…'

'Yes, Pietro. Go on.'

'I did my best, lad. I'd have gladly burned in hell if I could have got my knife into him. But there were too many of them…'

The shocked nun bent anxiously over the bed. 'Signor, he must not be excited into saying things like this.'

Pietro was dying as he had lived. His eyes shifted, blazed ferociously at her. 'Go away, woman. Go away and let men talk…'

A lump in Michael's throat was choking him. Pietro paused, fighting for air. Death was like a tiger trying to tear his spirit away but he clung on fiercely. 'I couldn't get her to leave the island. But you could, a smart young cockerel like you. Won't you do it for me, lad? Won't you take her away … or at least give her your protection?'

A man can wrestle with a decision for days. And then suddenly, in seconds, it has to be made. Pietro's bony hand tightened.

'Answer me, lad. I haven't long... Will you do it?'

Michael took a deep breath. 'Yes. If she'll go I'll take her.'

'And if she won't go. What then, lad?'

'Then I'll stay and protect her. I promise.'

'On the Holy Cross?'

'On the Holy Cross, Pietro.'

There was only one way such a promise could be kept, and from the way the old man's voice rang with triumph Michael was certain he knew it. 'How the mongrel will snarl and yelp. Ah, *Dio,* to live to see it...' Then, still sneering at death, he allowed himself to be dragged away. Michael had to lower his head again to hear his last words. 'Bless you, lad. Bless you both and make you happy...'

His eyes were empty again when Michael rose. The nun, her sweet face troubled, made the sign of the cross over his bed. 'It is not right he goes to his death with these thoughts of revenge. Pray for him, signor – he will need all our prayers.'

Michael had other views but did not express them. 'Has Miss Delfano been to see him again?'

'Oh, yes, signor. All last night and again this morning until she had to go to the school.'

'Did he recognise her?'

'Only once.'

At the door Michael paused and glanced back. The old fisherman was motionless on the bed, his face like yellow parchment. Michael tried to speak, shook his head, and walked quickly down the passage. At the entrance he turned to the nun.

'Does he have any relations on the island, sister?'

'No, signor. We haven't been able to trace any.'

'If there is any help I can give – no matter what it is – please let me know immediately. I am staying in La Primula hotel.'

'You are very kind, signor. Goodbye.'

Michael walked slowly along the cobbled waterfront, hardly noticing Mario and the fisherman who rose from a café table and followed him. Mixed with his grief for Pietro was a profound sense of gratitude to the old man for ending once and for all his vacillations. Now there would be no question of leaving Cristina, of facing a future full of regret and self-recriminations, for he knew full well the implications of his promise. Whether she would accept him in marriage – whether she would agree to leave the island if she did – he could not tell, but one thing was crystal clear: the decision opened out an entire new field of possibilities, and to exploit those possibilities he had to see her again. Somehow, then, in spite of her resisting it almost as much as Sabastian, he had to arrange another meeting.

His first move on reaching the hotel was to see the manager, Signor Martorella. Martorella was a plump, inoffensive little man with a tonsure like a monk and a permanent expression of benevolent anxiety.

'Yes, signor. At your service. What can I do for you?'

'I've decided to stay on a few more days and would like to keep my room. For four days at least – possibly more.'

The balance of emotion in Martorella's expression tipped heavily towards anxiety. 'You are not taking the ship this afternoon, then, signor?'

There was danger here… Michael had been expecting it and casually drew notes from his wallet. 'No. I'll be here at least another four days. To make certain my foreign currency comes out right I thought I'd pay you for them in advance.'

It worked as he had hoped. Martorella hesitated, sighed, and pulled himself together. He motioned briskly at the pale-faced youth at the desk. 'The signor is staying on another four days, Gino, and wishes to pay in advance. Make out an account for him.'

Relieved, Michael went upstairs to his

room and out on the balcony. The sun was shining again, but a slate grey bank of clouds was massing over the southern headlands. The air, heavy with humidity, made the sun burn with an unnatural fierceness.

As he stood there a woman carrying a large straw shopping basket came out of the hardware shop on his left and started across the piazza. There was no mistaking her determined walk or the severeness of her raven black hair. It was Maria, going across to the morning market.

It was a chance and Michael snatched it eagerly. He ran downstairs, saw to his satisfaction that no one was at the desk and called the hardware shop on the phone. 'Hello. Is that you, Signor Delfano?'

Carlo's voice betrayed immediate apprehension. '*Si, signor.* Who is that?'

'It's Michael Forbes. I've something very important to ask you. Will you come round to the hotel as soon as you can?'

'What is it about, signor? My daughter, Tina?'

'Yes. That's why I must see you alone. When can you come?'

A hush followed in which Michael could hear Carlo's heavy, troubled breathing. His hand tightened on the receiver. By this time the shopkeeper would have heard of the fight in Sabastian's office and would know of the constant watch being kept on him.

Carlo could not hope to avoid being seen entering the hotel, and there was real danger of Sabastian putting two and two together.

Michael broke the silence. 'It's very important, signor – something that might solve all Cristina's problems. Otherwise I wouldn't ask you. When is the earliest you can come?'

'I might have been able to come this afternoon, signor,' Carlo muttered. 'My wife is going out to see a friend… But it may not be before three o'clock and your ship sails soon after that…'

'Don't worry about the ship – I'm not going on it. That's one of the things I want to talk to you about.'

Carlo made no effort now to hide his apprehension. 'Not going, signor? Does Tina know this?'

'No. And perhaps it might be as well if you say nothing about it until I've seen you. You will come round this afternoon then?'

'Yes; after my wife has gone out I can perhaps come round for a few minutes. But I must not be seen with you, signor – you understand that.'

'Quite. I'm just as anxious we're not seen together. Come straight to my room, number ten. We'll talk in there and you leave alone. You'll say nothing to your wife about this, of course.'

Carlo's protest came from the heart.

'*Santa Maria,* no. And I beg you to be careful, signor. Trust nobody.'

'I'll be very careful. And I'll look forward to seeing you about three this afternoon.'

Michael returned to his room. So far things had gone well, but he had no illusions of the problems ahead. Carlo might be a potential ally; he might also live too much in fear of his wife's tongue to be trustworthy. And the most baffling problem – a safe meeting place where he could meet Cristina and have the time to put his proposition before her – remained as insoluble as before.

He gave it thought for over an hour and got nowhere. In desperation, arguing that boldness might succeed where caution failed, he even thought of asking her to come to his room; but when he remembered Martorella's troubled face he knew the risks were too great. Sabastian would certainly have considered the possibility, have warned the manager, and would not hesitate to have Cristina followed if she were allowed into the hotel. And failure was something Michael dared not risk. Physical danger apart, he knew that another violent scene would utterly end any chance of seeing her again.

The meeting place had to be completely safe, safe even from freakish accidents such as had happened in the cove. Restlessly he lit a cigarette and wandered out on the balcony again. The sky had hazed over and the sun was a white-hot ball overhead. Far out in the bay a cormorant drew his eyes, a tiny, elongated speck sweeping southwards over the waves. As it suddenly plunged into the sea his hands gripped the rails tightly. He stood motionless for a long moment, then drew in a deep breath. When he threw his cigarette away and turned back to the room there was both hope and excitement in his eyes.

CHAPTER 16

Carlo was late that afternoon. The ship in the bay had given three warning blasts on its siren and the boats clustered around it were pulling away when his bowed figure in his old black suit came hurrying down the cobbled pavement to the hotel. Michael, standing well back and to one side of his balcony to avoid being seen by his shadowers below, withdrew and went into the corridor outside. To his relief it was empty when Carlo appeared at the head of the stairs. Neither spoke until they were in the bedroom with the door closed behind them.

Carlo, blowing a little, sank gratefully into the chair Michael offered him. 'My pardon, signor, for being so late. But with women one can never tell… My wife did not leave until just before four o'clock.'

'It doesn't matter,' Michael told him. 'I suppose those two men of Sabastian's saw you come in?'

'I'm afraid so, signor. And I saw Sabastian himself leaving the jetty as I came out of the shop. He will be wondering why you have not gone on the ship today.'

Michael's face was grim. 'He'll be wondering, all right. There's probably quite a conference going on at this moment.'

Carlo's liquid brown eyes were troubled. 'Why did you not go, signor? It would have been the wisest thing to do. They are very dangerous men.'

'That's what I want to talk to you about. But first let me offer you a glass of wine. My friend left a bottle of Aleatico behind.'

Carlo showed interest. 'The best of the Elba wines, signor… Thank you – I would like a glass.'

Michael studied Carlo's face as he opened the bottle and filled two glasses. He could see what Cristina had told him was true – that once Carlo had been a very handsome man. Never strong in character perhaps – that had been her childhood impression retained in womanhood – but with a fire and temper that must once have passed as strength. But Sabastian's siege on his shop following his first wife's death had quenched that fire and this was the Carlo that remained: a sad man and, from all Michael's impressions, a kindly man. But also a weak man and therefore probably subject to many of the vacillations of the weak. Under Maria's thumb as he was, it was going to be difficult to decide how far he would go in defying her.

Carlo's hand reached out eagerly for the glass of wine Michael offered him, but his old-world courtesy kept it from his lips until Michael was comfortably seated.

'*Alla salute, signor.* Your good health and happiness.'

He controlled his eagerness well, rolling the wine around his mouth and clucking his appreciation. 'A good wine, signor. An excellent wine.'

As Michael offered him a cigarette Carlo half-opened his mouth to speak, took another sip of wine, and then leaned awkwardly forward in his chair. 'Signor, before you commence there is something I would like to say to you.'

Michael nodded, waited.

'My wife was very rude to you in the shop yesterday, signor and I owe you an apology for it. I would ask you to forgive her, however, because there are reasons for her behaviour...' Here Carlo was torn between loyalty to Maria and his pride, and to his great credit loyalty won. 'Since you and Tina met a few things have happened to distress her. Little things, of course, but you know how women worry...'

'What sort of things?' Michael asked sharply.

Carlo waved a distressed hand at his concern. 'Only little things, signor. A creditor here and there – they have pressed me for quicker payment... Nothing serious – but as I say, women worry. Please understand me, signor – I only mention this so you may find it easier to forgive Maria.'

Michael felt warmth for this weak but loyal man. 'There's no need to apologise. I'm only too sorry that I've made things worse for you.'

Carlo sighed and took another sip of wine. 'The fault isn't yours, signor. Maria is a good woman, but because she has to buy the food and mend the clothes she sees things differently from us. Her way would be for Tina to marry Sabastian and then shape him into another man, as a woman's sharp tongue can sometimes do. I have argued with her, but even I sometimes wonder if she is not right. For this way the poor child loses all and gains nothing.'

Michael had heard enough to be certain on whose side Carlo's real sympathies lay and decided to put his cards on the table.

'Tina doesn't need to lose so much; all she has to do is get away from this island. Has she told you I've tried to persuade her to go?'

Carlo flinched. 'No, signor.'

'Well, I have tried, damned hard. But she won't hear of leaving because of you and Giuseppe; she says you need her help too badly.' As Carlo's eyes dulled in shame he went on quietly. 'She wouldn't have told me all this if we hadn't been very close to one another, signor. But we're in love. She won't have told you that either, I suppose?'

Carlo lifted his worried face. 'No, signor. But I have known – that is why I was so ashamed yesterday. For love is a thing no woman can hide, and I have seen it shining out of Tina's face since the first day she met you.'

There was a long, troubled silence. Ash fell from Carlo's cigarette and rolled un-heeded down the greenish-black lapel of his suit. He gave a sigh of shame. 'I am a selfish old man, signor. I will try to persuade her to go… Perhaps there is a chance now that she has met you…'

Michael shook his head impatiently. 'No. I'd value your efforts to persuade her, of course, but as things stand at the moment I'm certain she wouldn't agree. After my fight with Sabastian yesterday and the threats he made, she refused point-blank to see me again. I want you to talk her into changing her mind. Tell her I have an en-tirely new idea that might free you all from this persecution, and that I must discuss it with her as soon as possible.'

Something of his enthusiasm entered Carlo. 'May I hear this new idea, signor?'

Michael hesitated. Apart from a natural desire to keep his proposal of marriage a secret until he made it himself, he feared a premature disclosure of his plans relating to it might give time for new doubts to enter Cristina's mind before he could refute them.

'I'd rather not discuss it until I see her, signor. But it is something that might revolutionise the whole problem – I can assure you of that. It isn't going to be easy to persuade her to see me. You'll have to work very hard on her, assure her that I'll be quite safe and Sabastian will hear nothing about it.'

Carlo looked troubled again. 'How can I assure her of that? With Sabastian's men trailing you like hounds and the island so small, where can you go without being seen by somebody? You have tried it before and found it impossible.'

Michael checked him. 'I've thought of a place. It isn't easy to reach and it isn't comfortable, but it is one place where we can be certain no one will come and find us.'

Carlo frowned his puzzlement. 'You have the advantage of me, signor. Where is there such a place on Veronia?'

Michael reached out for the shopkeeper's

glass to fill it. 'It's quite simple. In the Grotto. The Grotto of Tiberius.'

Carlo's melancholy face went suddenly pale. 'You can't be serious, signor.'

Michael lifted his eyes. 'I'm very serious. It's the one safe place on the island.'

'But surely you have heard the stories about it? It is an evil place – people on the island do not go there...'

Michael nodded. 'Exactly. And so it's the ideal place for us.' He offered Carlo the new-filled glass of wine. 'Surely you don't believe these stories about its being haunted.'

Carlo shifted uneasily, took a deep sip of wine before answering. 'There is seldom smoke without fire, signor. And many lives have been lost around the Grotto.'

Michael smiled at him. 'Cristina has been inside it before, you know. More than once.'

'I know – she went twice when she was a child. But I spanked her hard for it and told her never to go there again.'

'I went into it myself the other day,' Michael told him. 'It hasn't a pleasant atmosphere – I'll give you that – but there's nothing dangerous about it. There isn't even any risk from the sea if one is careful.' His voice became grim as he pursued his argument. 'The point is – if we take precautions in going there we will be safe from Sabastian and his men. And they are flesh and blood, not imaginary ghosts and goblins.'

Carlo lifted a handkerchief to mop his sweating forehead. 'You may be right, signor, but old superstitions die hard. In my time I have heard some terrible stories about the Grotto: for centuries it has been believed an evil place.' A shudder ran through him and involuntarily he crossed himself. 'I do not like the idea of my daughter going there, signor. It frightens me.'

Michael left him no escape. 'This persecution can't be allowed to go on any longer, signor. Cristina's not made of iron and sooner or later she must crack. Tell me of another place as safe as the Grotto and I'll be willing enough to go there instead. But it must be safe. I won't get a second chance of seeing her.'

Carlo mopped his forehead again. 'There is no other place safe from interference – I know that. If Martorella let her enter here they would follow her, and I dare not let you use my home...'

'Then what's the point in arguing about it? Both Cristina and I have been in the Grotto; we both know there's nothing to be afraid of. You must ask her, signor. After our experience in the cove she won't see me anywhere else – I know it. And if I don't get this last chance of seeing her then God knows what will happen to you all.'

Carlo lifted his hands in defeat. 'I will ask her. Tell me what you want me to say.'

'Tell her I have an entirely new idea that might change everything and I must see her. Point out there isn't any danger of anyone stumbling across us inside the Grotto and that we'll meet inside it. I feel almost certain they won't follow her if she goes out alone – she often goes for walks that way – and I'll shake anyone off who follows me. Ask her to go there as soon as possible – this evening if she can. Any time will suit me as long as I know an hour or two in advance.'

'If she agrees, how will I get in touch with you, signor?'

'I suggest you either phone me or drop a letter in the hotel. Perhaps a letter would be better,' Michael corrected, remembering the youth at the desk. 'I'll stay nearby until I hear from you.'

Carlo pulled out his watch, a massive old timepiece attached to his waistcoat by a silver chain, and gave a start. '*Mamma mia*, I must unlock the shop before Maria gets back...' He drained his glass with regret and rose. 'You shall hear from me, signor. But don't expect an answer too quickly. She is a stubborn girl and it may be difficult to make her agree.'

'Use all your influence on her,' Michael urged, accompanying him to the door. 'It's vitally important to us all. And if she still won't agree, then tell her I shan't hesitate to stop her in the street, thugs or no thugs. It's a cheap threat but I must see her.'

'I will do what I can, signor. But be patient and don't try to get in touch with me. You understand – one can be overheard on the telephone...'

'I'll wait,' Michael assured him. He opened the door, glanced out into the passage. It was empty and he motioned Carlo forward. 'Many thanks for coming, signor. Good luck.'

Carlo tip-toed out, voice hushed. 'I will do my best, signor. *Arrivederci.*'

Carlo hurried down the hotel staircase, his movements as fussy and furtive as an aged cockerel. At the top of the verandah steps he stared anxiously around. To his relief Mario and a fisherman were to the right of the hotel, playing cards in the shade of an alley. Seeing the fisherman touch Mario's arm he hurried quickly down the steps and towards his shop. In his concern he did not notice Maria until he was almost on her.

She was standing outside the shop doorway, hands on hips. He halted with a start, impaled on her sharp, challenging eyes.

'Where have you been?'

He half-opened his mouth to explain, realised he could not, and stared at her in dismay.

She strode up to him and sniffed his breath suspiciously. 'You've been drinking! You've been drinking in the hotel!'

'Only two glasses, Mamma. It was some-one I had to see.' By nature Carlo was not a liar, but he decided desperate situations called for desperate measures. 'It was a busi-ness matter, Mamma. A traveller I had to see.'

'A traveller, indeed. What was his name?'

Carlo floundered further into his own net. 'His name, Mamma...? Morelli. Antonio Morelli.'

Maria's formidable bosom swelled threat-eningly. 'You realise that I can check this by looking in the guest book or by asking the manager...?' Seeing Carlo's expression her temper broke. 'It was unlucky for you that my friend happened to be out this after-noon, wasn't it? *Santa Maria*, I have only to turn my back for a few minutes and you are out guzzling wine. Is there any wonder we live like dogs in a kennel?'

Two women passed them. One nudged the other, who gave a titter of amusement. Carlo tried to withdraw the quarrel from the public domain by edging for the shop doorway. 'I haven't missed any business, Mamma. There is no trade in the afternoons. We might just as well close down until five o'clock...'

She followed him into the shop. 'So now you want to close so you can drink wine in the afternoons too... A traveller indeed. Who was it you met in there – that old winebag Doretti? Tell me! I want to give him a piece of my mind when I see him.'

Carlo closed the door, but a listener in the sunlight outside could have heard her voice for long minutes, questioning and scourging him like a torturer's whip.

CHAPTER 17

The threatened break in the weather came the following day, making Veronia a different island. A driving wind swept off the sea and the sky was bleak with slate grey clouds. Although rain did not fall before the morning market closed, the island women were subdued both in their chatter and their appearance as they huddled around the stalls in mackintoshes and head scarves. Behind them the sea was no longer blue but steel grey and angry, with waves that dashed over the waterfront and ran in rivulets among the cobblestones. The sun-worshipping pigeons of the piazza, hiding in the eaves of shops and warehouses, cocked apprehensive eyes at the clouds and huddled their heads deeper into their puffed-up feathers.

Michael found the hotel, with its white-washed walls and thin windows, a bleak and draughty place without sunlight. One of his first tasks that morning was to phone the hospital, when he learned with grief that Pietro had died late the previous evening without recovering consciousness. He also learned Cristina had been with him to the end, and for a moment wondered if a precious opportunity of seeing her had been missed – an opportunity Pietro himself would have been the first to encourage. His tensed exasperation slowly eased when he realised they would not have been alone together. But her attendance at the hospital did mean one thing – that it was highly unlikely Carlo would have had a chance of speaking to her when she eventually returned home. And that could mean another twenty-four hours of waiting before he received her reply.

The thought made his heart sink. He had already read the few books he had brought with him, and with nothing to occupy his fretting mind the minutes passed like hours. In the early afternoon steady rain began to fall, and the only consolation he could find as he stared disconsolately out into the piazza, was that the two oil-skinned fishermen huddled in a shop doorway were waiting in less favourable conditions than he.

His surprise, then, was all the greater when just before two o'clock the hotel manager's son, Gino, brought an unstamped letter up to his room, telling him it had been found in the post box with the afternoon mail.

Michael closed the door before opening the envelope. Inside it was a ruled piece of paper that looked as if it had been hastily torn from one of Carlo's account books. Michael paused a second with it in his hand. He had no illusions: if Cristina's reply were negative his chances of seeing her again were slim indeed. The message was short, hastily printed in pencil.

Dear Signor Forbes,
My daughter has agreed to meet you in the place of your choice but is not yet certain when she can go, although she hopes it may be possible this evening. When she knows for certain I will drop another note into the hotel.
I beg you to be very careful, signor.
Carlo Delfano

Tension eased on Michael's face as he read and re-read the message. He was to get his last chance; now everything rested on his making the most of it. To be certain of being ready when her second message came he began making his preparations.

Later that same day Cristina stood gazing from her bedroom window over the piazza.

Rain was still beating steadily down, splashing among the myriads of tiny pools that lay among the cobblestones. Out at sea the early evening sky was darkened into a storm light, through which a single ray of sunshine shone like a shaft of white fire before the clouds closed sullenly again. The wind had a restless sound, buffeting the window and moaning among the eaves.

The girl's face was marked with grief and fear. The previous day, because of her presence at Pietro's side, she had only heard of Michael's decision to remain on Veronia in the late evening, and by that time grief at Pietro's approaching death had served to dilute her fear. But today it was like a baying bloodhound, never allowing her mind a moment's rest in which to wonder at this final proof of his love for her. He must know that Sabastian would take this as the throwing down of the gauntlet – what was his plan, then, to counter the attack that must inevitably fall on him? Or had he no plan; was it just a dogged act of defiance?

She felt she could wait no longer to hear: that she must establish some kind of quick contact with him. There was the telephone, and if she could have been certain that the hotel staff (or, for that matter, the girl on the exchange) were to be trusted, she would have used it. But as things were a phone call from her might well precipitate the explosion she feared.

The answer to her problem came unexpectedly. There was a tap on her door and Giuseppe entered. He was wearing a chequered shirt and jeans, and as usual his fair hair was tousled. He slouched in with his teenage air of embarrassed nonchalance and gave her an apologetic grin.

'Can you lend me the money for a packet of fags until pay day, Tina? I'm flat broke.'

She nodded nervously and fumbled in her handbag. As he took the money from her he nodded at the stairs through the open door. 'Any idea what's wrong with the old man tonight? He isn't sick, is he?'

She looked up anxiously. 'I don't think so. Why?'

Giuseppe shrugged. 'I went down to ask him if he'd lend me the money and had to speak to him three times before he heard me. And then he stared at me as if I were a ghost or something. I gave it up and came to you.'

'Is he alone?'

'Yes. Didn't you hear Maria telling him she was going out tonight to see the friend she missed yesterday?'

Cristina went to the door. 'I'd better go down and see what's wrong.'

Giuseppe checked her. 'How's Michael getting on? Any more news?'

She shook her head.

221

Giuseppe's voice was grudgingly admiring. 'He can't value his hide very much. I'd still be running if I'd taken a swipe at Sabastian. I suppose he's got the sense to stay inside the hotel?'

'I don't know – that's what worries me...' It was then the idea came to her, and she turned eagerly towards the youth. 'Peppi, you can help me here. You're friendly with most of Sabastian's men – if you handle it right you ought to be able to find out what Michael's doing without getting him into any trouble.'

Giuseppe eyed her doubtfully. 'You mean you want me to have a word with him?'

'No; at least not if it means the slightest risk to you both. But you could find out if he's keeping indoors and how long he has booked to stay – things like that. You know the manager's son quite well, don't you?'

'Sure. I know Gino all right.'

'Then go and help me. Find out all you can. But don't do anything that might get either of you into danger. Don't let anyone think you're being curious on my behalf, for example. If necessary let them think you don't like him; that you wish he hadn't stayed. You know the way to handle it.'

Giuseppe gave her the benefit of his worldly wisdom. 'That won't be so hard – I think you're crazy to prefer him to Sabastian. What has he got, anyway?'

She gave him a push. 'Never mind. Go and find out all you can. But be careful – promise me that.'

Giuseppe slouched out, hiding his pleasure at having her trust under a mask of teenage indifference. 'All right, all right. I'll see what I can do.'

She waited until he had left the house and then went downstairs to her father, who was in the sitting-room behind the shop. It was a room filled with massive pieces of old-fashioned furniture, with a single window that overlooked a tiny cobbled enclosure that was their back garden. Even in good weather it was a room that never made sunlight welcome; tonight it was as grey and gloomy as the heavy rain outside.

Her father, wearing felt slippers and his black smoking jacket, was sitting in his armchair near the window. His head was slumped forward, making her believe for the moment that he was asleep.

'Father,' she called softly.

Accustomed now to the twilit room she saw his eyes were open and staring at the empty, embossed stove in front of him. At her voice he seemed to go rigid, as though caught in a furtive act. Anxiously she approached him.

'Peppi said he thought you weren't well. Is anything the matter?'

The glance he threw her was full of guilt,

shifting away the moment it touched her. 'No, *cicci*. I am just resting, that is all.'

She knew something was wrong. At any other time he would have taken advantage of Maria's absence and gone to the wine shops with his friends. She went up to his chair. 'Are you certain you're feeling all right?'

As she spoke she reached out to stroke his cheek. It was a familiar caress of hers and he, after enjoying it for a few seconds, would always turn and kiss her hand. But tonight as she touched him he turned his face sharply away.

For a moment the very foundations of her life seemed to shiver. She had seen him decay, she had seen their fortunes go from bad to worse, but his love for her – that she had taken as much for granted as her eyes and heart. Nothing could harm it: it was outside mischief and outside sorrow. It was the great hidden reef over which the sea could pound for ever.

Yet now he had turned away from her hand. She dropped on her knees beside him. 'Father! What is it? What have I done?'

He kept his face averted from her. She saw it was working in grief and tried to pull him round to face her. 'Father, what have I done? You must tell me...'

'It's nothing you have done, *cicci*. You must not think that...'

'Then what is it? What has happened?'

224

When he did not answer she threw her arms around him. With her head against his chest she could feel the deep trembling of his body. Frightened she lifted up her face. 'What is it, Father? Is it Sabastian again?'

He shook his head, unhappily. The trembling of his body grew. Suddenly he gave a great sob.

'Oh, *cicci*. Oh, my little *bambina...*'

She pressed closer to him. His body was racked with sobs now, like an engine that had torn from its bearings. She reached for his face and felt the scald of tears on her hand.

'Look at me,' she whispered. 'Why won't you look at me?'

'Because I am so ashamed, *cicci*... To do this to you... I shall never forgive myself. Never...'

'But what have you done?'

'I have deceived you, *cicci*. You who are everything in the world to me.'

'How have you deceived me? I don't understand.'

Shame and misery broke his voice. 'It was yesterday afternoon, *cicci*, in the hotel... Your young friend, the Englishman, begged me to speak to you and arrange a meeting... He said it was urgent, that he had a new idea for you that might change everything. I agreed to do it, but on my way back I met Maria. She thought I had been drinking and quarrelled with me...'

He paused, struggled to pull a handkerchief from his trouser pocket. He kept his face averted as he dabbed his eyes and blew his nose.

'And then,' Cristina asked anxiously. 'What happened then?'

'*Cicci*, you know what Maria is like. Her tongue – *Santa Maria*, it nearly drove me crazy. I dared not tell her the truth; I said I had been talking to a traveller called Morelli. So what did she do – she went over to the hotel, found there was no such man, and started the quarrel all over again by accusing me of speaking to your friend. I tried to keep silent, *cicci* – I swear it – but something happens inside me when she shouts like that and I found myself explaining to her what had happened.'

Cristina was looking puzzled. 'You say all this happened yesterday. Then why haven't you given me his message yet?' As Carlo rocked his head in shame her voice sank into a whisper. 'Maria told you to say nothing. Is that what you're telling me?'

He nodded brokenly. 'She said that nothing but misery could come of it, that if we went on giving encouragement to the Englishman Sabastian would close us down. And it is true, *cicci* – I cannot go on much longer. Bills, bills, they are everywhere... But Maria said something else too. She asked me if I realised

I might never see you again if Michael took you away. And, *cicci*, I suddenly realised what hell life would be here without you...' At that Carlo broke down completely, clutching her as if she were already on the point of leaving.

'You mustn't be so upset,' she whispered. 'I understand, and I'm not angry with you.'

'Oh, *cicci*, what has happened to me...? I break my promise to Michael... I put my selfish feelings before you... I even break my promise to Maria... *Santissima Madonna,* what would your sweet mother think of me now?'

Her eyes were wet as she comforted him. 'Don't worry about it any more. Just try to remember what Michael said to you.'

'He said he wanted to discuss this new idea with you as soon as possible, and for a meeting place suggested the Grotto. I had to find out when you would go and send a message back to him'

She gave a start. 'The Grotto!'

'Yes, *cicci.* That was another reason I allowed Maria to persuade me... I do not want you to go there. But he said he had been inside it, that it was not dangerous, and it was the only place on the island where you could meet unseen.'

'The Grotto,' Cristina repeated. Excitement grew in her eyes a she stared at him. 'It is true – no one ever goes there.'

'But are you certain it is safe, *cicci?* There

227

have been so many terrible stories about it.'

She ignored his fears, glancing down at his watch. 'When can you get in touch with him? Tonight?'

Carlo looked startled. 'You're not thinking of going there now, in this weather.'

She was on her feet now, all nerves and eagerness. 'It may be too late to arrange for tonight – I don't know. But you must let him know I'm willing to go – otherwise he may do something rash. How were you going to give him my message? By phone?'

'No, *cicci*. By letter.'

She took his hands to pull him to his feet. 'Then write it now before Maria comes back. Quickly, and Giuseppe can deliver it.'

At that moment they heard footsteps in the passage way alongside the house. A moment later Giuseppe appeared, wearing a rain-soaked mackintosh. Cristina turned to him eagerly.

'What did you find out? Is he in the hotel now?'

Giuseppe shook his head. 'No. Gino said he went out over half an hour ago.'

The eagerness in her eyes suddenly turned to fear. 'Gone out! But where?'

Giuseppe shrugged as he flung off his mackintosh. 'Don't ask me. All Gino knows is that he went out dressed as though he were going for a long walk. Thick mackintosh, scarf, heavy shoes – the whole works.'

She swung round on her father. 'Are you sure you understood him properly? That he didn't want me to meet him in the Grotto tonight?'

Carlo shook his troubled face. 'No, *cicci*. He was hoping you might go tonight, but he was not going to do anything until he heard from me. How could he? The last thing you told him was that you wouldn't see him again.'

Giuseppe was eyeing them curiously. 'What's all this about the Grotto?'

She explained to him Michael's request, stressing the need for secrecy. Giuseppe whistled his astonishment. 'He must be keen!'

'Is that all you found out from Gino? Didn't he tell you how long Michael had booked to stay?'

'Four days at least. And there was something else. Gino found two letters for him in the hotel box this afternoon. One was with the afternoon post and the other came about four-thirty. Neither were stamped so someone on the island must have dropped them in. Gino says Michael looked pretty pleased with himself after getting them.'

A presentiment of danger ran through her like an electric current. 'He received two messages this afternoon and this evening he goes out dressed for a long walk...' She turned sharply towards Carlo. 'What else did Maria say to you? She didn't say she was going to tell Sabastian, did she?'

Carlo flinched and paled. '*Santa Maria,* no. All she wanted was the message to be kept from you so that Michael would grow discouraged and leave the island.'

'Are you certain of that? You hear what Giuseppe says – Michael received two letters this afternoon from someone on the island. Who else does he know here who would write to him?'

Fear was naked in Carlo's eyes now. 'What are you saying to me, *cicci?*'

'I'm not sure. But there's something wrong – I can feel it.' She ran from the room, to reappear a minute later in a mackintosh, head scarf, and a pair of thick shoes. 'I'm going out to look for him. I'll be back as soon as I can.'

Carlo ran after her. 'Wait, *cicci.* How can you go searching about for him in this weather?' When she did not answer he caught hold of her arm. 'If you must go, let me come with you. Let us both go.'

Giuseppe nodded and was reaching for his mackintosh again when Cristina checked him. If Sabastian were somehow involved his men would be involved too. And while they would not harm her they would have little respect for her menfolk if they interfered... 'No, I'd rather go alone. No, please – stay here. I'll be back as quickly as

I can.'

'*Cicci*, wait. Wait until Maria comes back. Then we might find out what is happening...'

She ran into the passage. The rain was cold on her face. The last thing she heard before closing the door was her father, his voice sobbing like the wind around her. 'Holy Mother, what have I done? What have I done to my little girl?'

CHAPTER 18

The rain was sweeping in from the leaden evening sky when Cristina ran into the piazza. She hesitated only a moment before making for the southern waterfront that ran to the cliffs. While she realised her fear could be imaginary, an instinct above reason told her there was a link between the letters Michael had received and the Grotto. And if it were true there was no time to waste, for he had left the hotel over half an hour ago. It was a thought that prevented her noticing the oilskin-clad figure who slipped out of a waiting lorry and followed her.

The waterfront was deserted, its warehouses empty and shuttered as she hurried along it. On her right grey waves hurled themselves at the sea wall and sent spray hissing down to the cobblestones, enlarging the pools made by the rain. Her haste allowed her no time to avoid them and soon her shoes were full of water.

The man following her glanced round, saw he had no witnesses, and ran lightly forward. The sound of the waves deadened his approach, and he was on her before she started and spun round.

It was Sabastian, disguised as a fisherman in a black oilskin and sou'wester. He took hold of her arm, pulling her towards a nearby warehouse. 'Come with me, *cara*. I want a word with you.'

Her mind was leaping ahead, trying to relate his surprise appearance to her news of Michael even as she tried to jerk her arm away. 'Let me go. Let go of my arm.'

'It's better you come with me, *cara*.' His free hand was fumbling with a key as he spoke, opening one of the warehouse doors. 'I've something very important to tell you.'

Feeling certain now that his appearance had some connection with Michael she did not put up the struggle she might otherwise have done. He stood aside, motioned her to enter the warehouse. When she hesitated he took hold of her arm again. 'Quickly, *cara*. Come inside out of the rain.'

He followed on her heels. In spite of the warehouse being pitch-black inside he closed the door immediately. She heard a scratching sound and a second later his face appeared in the flare of a match. Shading it with his hand he crossed over to a lantern hanging from a wooden beam. A moment later a yellow glow spread slowly through the darkness. She saw the walls around her were stacked high with empty fish crates. On the corrugated iron roof above the rain was beating fiercely.

Sabastian threw off the sou'wester and turned to her. She saw now that he appeared to be under considerable tension. His breathing was laboured and there were lines of strain round his dark eyes and swollen mouth.

'What is it you have to tell me?' she demanded. 'I haven't long, so please hurry.'

He gave her a slow smile, pulled out his cigarette case and offered it to her. When she jerked her head in refusal he shrugged and took a cigarette himself. There was a deliberation about his movements that both puzzled and alarmed her.

'I asked you what you want. Why are you looking at me like that?'

He sucked smoke deeply into his lungs, exhaled it through his narrow nostrils. 'Answer me a question instead, *cara*. Where were you going a moment ago? Surely not just for a walk?'

She stared at him angrily. 'You're not

telling me that's your reason for wanting to speak with me?'

His black eyes, alight with some strange fever, mocked her. 'Perhaps, *carissima*. Perhaps.'

Reviling herself for a fool she turned sharply for the door. He moved faster, leaping forward and putting his back to it.

Her heart was thudding heavily now. 'Let me go. You've no right to keep me in here like this.'

There was a peculiar abandonment in the smile he gave her, as if he had sold his soul to the devil and knew it. He turned the key in the lock and thrust it into the pocket of his oilskin. 'You're staying here with me, *carissima*. As long as I want you to stay.'

She was white to the lips now. 'There's a limit to what you can do, Sabastian, even on this island. And you'll have gone past it if you're not careful.'

He laughed mockingly, sauntered away and sat on a crate. A hammer lay on the hard-packed earthen floor; he picked it up and began thudding the ground with it, bringing up tiny spurts of brown dust. 'If you think I'm going to molest you, you can forget it. All I'm going to do is keep you here until I decide it's safe for you to go. So you needn't worry about your chastity.'

'But why? What's your reason?'

For a moment he did not answer, thudding the hammer viciously into the earth. Then he lifted up bitter eyes to her.

'Stop pretending, Tina. You thought you knew where your Englishman had gone tonight and you were going there after him. Did you think I wouldn't guess what was going on when Giuseppe went over to the hotel and talked to Gino?'

She knew now her suspicions must be right and her throat was dry with fear. 'Maria told you everything, didn't she? And you sent Michael those letters today. What was in them, Sabastian?'

He drove the hammer once more into the churned-up ground. His voice was low, mocking. 'Can't you guess, *cara?* You have heard what he wanted?'

'You sent him a false message from my father that I would be in the Grotto tonight.'

'You're clever, *cara.* And what did the second message say?'

The confirmation of her fears made her feel sick. 'I don't know about that. But I do know you sent your men out on the cliffs to wait for him.'

The mockery in his feverish eyes grew. 'Wrong this time, *cara.* He'll get into the Grotto without any trouble.'

His expression frightened her. 'You sent nobody! Why?'

He picked up the hammer again, studied it with mock interest. 'Perhaps because I wanted him to have a cold evening waiting for you. Perhaps that was why.'

She had the feeling he was speaking the truth and was bewildered. 'But what good will that do? He'll learn what has happened as soon as he gets back.'

He turned the hammer over in his hand. In the yellow lamplight the heavy bruises on his face made it look evil. 'Will he, *cara?* I wonder.'

As he spoke his eyes lifted to her. Only for a split second, but the glint in them brought her a greater fear than she had ever known before. There was something devilish here ... something she did not understand but which threatened Michael.

'What else have you done, Sabastian?' she breathed. 'Tell me. What is it?'

'I've told you, *cara* – nothing else. I've let him think you wanted to meet him in the Grotto tonight and I've taken precautions he'll be there alone. That is all. I'll swear it on the Bible if you want me to.'

A surge of relief brought anger with it. 'You don't think a childish trick like this is going to turn him against me, do you? All I have to do tomorrow is phone him and explain what happened.'

He smiled down at the hammer. 'Who knows what it might do, *cara?* Who knows?'

Anger made her voice into a whip which she swung at him. 'You must have lost your mind to believe such a thing. Michael's a man, not a spoiled, jealous child like you. If I were you I'd be afraid he might come round to your offices tomorrow and give you another thrashing.'

Her voice checked at his expression. For a moment his eyes were defenceless with shock as he lifted one hand to his face. His cheeks had paled and the bruises on them stood out in vivid relief. Then he cursed and drove the hammer viciously into the ground. *'Corpo di Cristo;* you mock me with it – and after I let him go...' He was shuddering with fury as he glared up at her. 'Do you really believe me a child, playing child's tricks? Don't you understand what is going to happen to him tonight?'

The return of fear smothered her voice into a whisper. 'Happen! What do you mean?'

'Haven't you heard of the legend of Tiberius? Have you forgotten the Grotto is haunted?'

The feverish, triumphant glitter in his eyes, the working of his bruised face, made her wonder for a moment if his mind had gone. 'You don't believe that legend any more than I do. You've been in the Grotto – you know it's not dangerous.'

His headshake was slow and deliberate. 'I've never said that, *cara*. I believe that sometimes it is the most dangerous place in the world. As it will be tonight.'

CHAPTER 19

All her premonitions were back, the blind fear that had been with her when she heard about the letter. 'You're joking, aren't you?' she whispered. 'You're saying this just to frighten me.'

He rose abruptly from the crate, as though escaping from the admonitions of his better self. In the lamplight his face was that of a stranger, abandoned and ruthless.

'I'm not joking, *cara*. I gave him his chance two days ago – even though he struck me in front of my own staff. I begged him to go... I begged you to make him go. When he did not, I knew the truth. It had to be he or me...'

Her face was dazed, incredulous. 'What are you saying to me? That he is going to be killed in the Grotto tonight?'

He stood motionless, without speaking, but the answer lay across his face like a disfiguring scar. Her voice rose hysterically. 'But how? You don't believe in the legend – you've told me so. Then what are you talking about? Have you gone mad or is there something else you know about it?'

The bright glitter of his eyes told her she

was right. 'What is it?' she breathed. 'What happens down there?'

In the silence that followed the wind outside could be heard moaning around the warehouse like a lost spirit. He lit another cigarette, bracing his hand to check its trembling. She was frantic now, seizing his arm and digging her fingers into the wet oilskin that covered it.

'Tell me what happens. What have you done to him?'

His swollen lips mocked her. 'I shall do nothing, *cara*. It is Tiberius who will take revenge on him, not I.'

'Stop talking like that. It's something you are doing. You don't believe in the legend any more than I do.'

'You are wrong there, *cara*. It is the Grotto that will kill him. That is what the whole island will say when they find out he went there, and it will be the truth.'

The yellow lamplight, his words, the drumming of the rain on the roof: it was suddenly all larger than life, the stuff nightmares are made of. 'How can the Grotto kill him? What is there in it that's so dangerous?' When he did not answer she went on frantically: 'If he dies it will be murder. You realise that, don't you?'

'Will it? He chose the Grotto as a meeting place. He is the big-headed, clever Englishman who thinks us a lot of superstitious peasants. I have done no more than let him think you are going there tonight.'

'But if the Grotto is dangerous, isn't that still murder?'

'If the fool wishes to die, why should I stop him?'

'Do you think you can get away with this? At my first opportunity I shall tell the police about the letters.'

'It will be your word against mine, *cara* – no one else knows I wrote them. And even if they believed you, how could they prove I knew I was sending him to his death? Courts of law don't take into account island superstitions.'

She brushed the sweat from her eyes, tried to take hold of the situation before it ran away to madness with them both. 'I don't know what's in the Grotto, but if it's dangerous to Michael you've got to rescue him. You can't murder a man just because he happens to fall in love with me. You're Sabastian, the boy I used to play with...' When he did not answer she dug her fingers into his arms again, shook him. 'Do you hear me? You can't murder an innocent man.'

He pushed her back and turned away. She followed him, fighting for Michael's life. 'What good can this do you? I'll never marry you, and even if you aren't punished by the law you'll have a murder on your conscience for the rest of your life.'

As he turned to face her it seemed for the moment that his better self had risen from the ground where he had discarded it and was struggling for possession of him. 'Once I said you had the power to drop me into hell, *cara,* and you laughed at me. Do you see now how true it is?'

'No woman is worth it, Sabastian. Don't do it. Get Michael away and neither of us will tell a soul what has happened. I promise you that.'

In the lamplight the hard lines of his face blurred as one self superimposed itself on the other in the grim battle to possess him. He brushed an arm across his forehead, wiping away the sweat that was forming there.

'You can't murder a man just because he is brave enough to defy you and your men, Sabastian. You'll never forgive yourself if you do – I know you too well for that.'

Memory and strain made his voice tremble. 'But he struck me, *carissima* ... in front of my staff. And he did not leave on the ship after I had warned him to go. Now people are talking ... soon they will be laughing. If it goes on the whole island will be laughing at me.'

'And which is worse? To be laughed at by a few fools when you know you are right, or to have a murder on your soul? In any case people won't laugh long – their memories are too poor.'

He moved away again, trying to escape from her pleading, but she gave him no respite. 'Please, Sabastian. For your sake as well as Michael's... Please hurry.'

He paused. 'For my sake?'

There is a place beyond revenge and she had long reached it. 'Why not? You were my friend once. You could be my friend again if you saved Michael.'

Her words were a mistake, their magnanimity giving a new hope to the receding devil within him. Once again his eyes had a fever in them as he turned to her.

'We could make a bargain, *cara*. If you'll promise to marry me I'll go straight to the Grotto and do everything in my power to save Michael. I swear it.'

The glitter in his eyes told her which way victory had gone, and her pleas choked in her throat. 'You'll bargain with an innocent man's life?'

'What do you expect me to do – help him so that he can take you away to England?' Eagerly he drew nearer to her. 'It is a fair offer, *cara*, but you must hurry. There may be little time left.'

Suspicion gave her a last, faint hope. 'You keep saying his life is in danger but you won't tell me the reason. Why is the Grotto sometimes the most dangerous place in the world? Why is it so dangerous tonight?'

He nodded and motioned her to keep quiet. In the silence she heard the moaning of the wind outside and the heavy beat of rain on the roof. 'What is it?' she breathed. 'What am I supposed to hear?'

'The rain, *carissimia*. Listen how it beats down. It came just at the right time to give me my idea.'

'But what has rain to do with the Grotto and Michael?'

His laugh mocked her. 'Don't you remember the legend – when clouds form and rain falls it means Tiberius is angry. And his anger means death to anyone in the Grotto.'

Again she had a feeling of unreality. 'What are you saying to me? Tell me quickly.'

'Then listen, *cara*, and you will understand.'

When he had finished her eyes were shocked with horror. 'But why doesn't anyone else know this? Why haven't you told anyone?'

She knew the answer before he gave it. 'Nobody fishes in the sea around those cliffs and it is rich, particularly in crayfish. Why should I share with others what I have learned for myself? They have eyes and brains too – let them use them.'

Nothing could have convinced her more that he was speaking the truth: she knew his own boat had often been seen near the headland. 'But it has been raining for hours … he could already be dead…' Something snapped in her mind and she found herself struggling with him, trying to beat his face with her fists. 'You're a devil … a murderer. *Santissima Madonna* – Michael may already be dead…'

His face was as pale as her own as he gripped her wrists and pulled her arms down. 'I was more patient with him than with any other man. I gave him chance after chance … even after he struck me … and the fool would not take them.'

In her torment she twisted, struggled, flung words at him like daggers. 'Chances! You never gave anyone a chance in your life. You're not a man at all – you're a *guappo* … a coward. And you want me to marry you…' Her voice cracked in a hysterical laugh. 'You! I'd rather marry the worst of your men. I'd rather marry Mario, with his stinking breath… He's only a rat but you're a devil.'

She could have said nothing worse to him. Her wrists felt as if they would snap as he dragged her closer.

'No one speaks to me that way. No one – not even you. You'll do as I say – you'll marry me or the Englishman will die tonight.'

Paradoxically his very threat gave her fresh hope and a greater degree of control. 'How can you be sure he isn't already dead?'

'I can't – at least not with certainty. But other times when it has rained as heavily it has taken over eight hours to happen.'

She tried to remember exactly when it had commenced raining that day and found she could not. 'When did it begin today?'

'Just after noon, although not very heavily for the first two hours.'

Noon! And it was not yet eight o'clock… Sudden hope blazed in her eyes. 'There's still a chance – you know there is. If we take a car or lorry down to the cliffs we might still be in time. Hurry, Sabastian. For God's sake, hurry.'

He did not move, his bruised face a cruel mask in the lamplight. 'Aren't you forgetting something, *carissima?* Haven't you a promise to make me first?'

At the locked door she turned back, her voice low but intense. 'Don't make me do it, Sabastian – for both our sakes. I should make your life hell, every minute of the day and night. I would – I promise it. In six months you would hate me more than I hate you.'

His laughter mocked her. 'You say that now – it will be different then.' He motioned upwards., 'Hurry, *carissima.* Tiberius's men may be already on their way. Every wasted second could mean his death.'

On the corrugated-iron roof the rain was thrumming down like the roll of drums before an execution. She knew she had no choice and hesitated no longer. 'Very well. Get Michael safely from the Grotto, don't interfere with him again while he is on the island, and I'll marry you.'

His face became alive with exultation. 'You swear it, Tina? On the Holy Mother?'

'On the Holy Mother,' she said bitterly.

Instantly his movements became feverish in their haste. He snatched up his sou'wester from a nearby crate. 'I have one of my lorries in the piazza,' he muttered. 'It'll be quicker to take it than to fetch my car.'

'I'm coming with you,' she told him. 'I want to be certain he is safe.'

He did not argue and unlocked the door. A cold gust of wind blew in on them. The lantern threw a yellow stain into the gloom, shone on the pencil-straight rain lancing down. He motioned her outside as he blew out the light. She ran through the door, her feet sinking into a pool of water. He slammed the door and followed her, running down the deserted, rain-swept waterfront.

CHAPTER 20

Michael paused in his climb round the headland. Below him the grey sea, laced with foam, surged sullenly against the rocks. Behind him, bleak and forbidding, the cliffs towered up into the leaden sky. Seeing no one was following him he turned to resume his climb, the wind tugging at his drenched mackintosh and sweeping the rain into his face.

He did not find the approach to the Grotto as easy as on his last visit, the rain making the rocks treacherous, and he had two painful falls before reaching a broader rock-shelf that ran downwards round the headland. Here the going was easier and a minute later he stood within sight of the Grotto.

With its entrance wet and dripping it reminded him more than ever of a gaping rapacious mouth. The waves, sucked in and ejected as rapidly through the deep gully, were like the licking tongue of some mythical monster, long-denied a victim and now seeing one almost within its grasp.

He paused at the entrance. On his last visit he had noticed the apparent power of the

Grotto to resist light; tonight it was as black as the inside of a tomb. He pulled out a torch from his mackintosh pocket and then paused. The headland covered him on the southern flank, but to the north he could be seen from the cliffs. He found it a real effort of will to step forward unaided into the darkness.

The chill of the Grotto sank into him and he noticed again its peculiar earth-like smell. The wind did not follow him inside, although its dull booming against the head-land above seemed to accentuate the hungry swish and obscene gurgling of the water in the gully. Judging himself safe now from observation he switched on the torch.

The beam ripped great strips of light from the darkness with an audacity that was frightening. He saw the lichen-stained walls again, the grotesque patches of dried seaweed and the wave-swept gully. Before he had time to start forward the blackness above him exploded into life with a great rustle of dry wings. A shadow, enormously enlarged by his torch, swooped crazily across the opposite wall, followed instantly by another. Something flew angrily at his head. Heart hammering with shock he ducked and felt the cold draught of wings. Through the swish of waves and the boom of wind he became conscious of a high-pitched piping that stabbed his ears like needles. Shining his torch upwards he saw a frantic swarm of bats veer away like a black cloud and flee down the Grotto. The rustle of their wings settled slowly as he swung his torch away, but their needle-thin squealing was a reminder of their fury at his intrusion.

The shock had jangled nerves already tightened by the eeriness of the Grotto, and he frowned at the trembling of his hands as he lit a cigarette. He found a rock-shelf near the gully and sat down. Rain had soaked through his mackintosh, chilling his shoulders. He threw the mackintosh off and glanced at his watch. It was seven-fifteen. He was in good time – the second letter had told him to be in the Grotto by seven-thirty, although it had given a warning that Cristina might be late and he was to wait for her arrival.

The black water of the gully ebbed and flowed. He shone his torch into it and instantly it turned green and bottomless. Nameless things shone up at him like avid eyes. He drew back sharply as the splash of a larger wave touched his face like a cold hand.

As the chill of the Grotto sank deeper into him he was forced to put on his mackintosh again. Sitting there he had the feeling a thousand hating eyes were watching him. He listened, and again heard the needle-thin squealing of the bats. He could imagine they were huddled blackly together, sharp teeth exposed, waiting for a signal to swoop down and destroy him.

Suppressing a shudder he glanced at his watch again. Seven-twenty – in a few minutes more he would go outside to look for Cristina. To save the battery he switched off his torch. Instantly darkness swooped on him, pressing on all sides. He felt disembodied, a spirit lost in the depths of Erebus. The smell of wet earth and decay became suddenly stronger than before; it seemed to blow on his face from the rear of the Grotto as if some creature of darkness were stirring in its lair. Switching on the torch quickly he swung it round, but could see nothing except the black hole into which the waves flowed and ebbed. The squealing of the bats, which had quietened for a moment, grew in fury again as he left the torch burning.

Just before seven-thirty he rose. In spite of the fierce wind and driving rain outside it was a relief beyond measure to leave the Grotto. He made his way round the headland corner, but although there was still enough light for him to search the rain-swept cliffs he could see nothing of Cristina. The temptation to stay outside on the rocks was strong, but he knew the risk of being observed was not worth taking. Reluctantly he turned and went back.

In the next fifteen minutes he made two further trips outside without success and began reconciling himself to a long wait. By this time the atmosphere of the Grotto was making his thoughts more and more fanciful. He began comparing his and Cristina's plight with that of the long-dead lovers, and it became increasingly difficult to avoid identifying himself with them. For in two thousand years nothing had changed in the Grotto – the sea was as cruel and the darkness as full of demons…

Once more the smell of decay and wet earth moved like an evil draught down the gully. A heavy gust of wind boomed and shrieked round the headland above. When it had passed he thought he heard a scrabbling sound on the rocks. For a moment shock held him motionless. Then he switched on the torch and shone it down the gully. Seeing nothing he swung the beam around. As it shone on the incoming waves and the ledge alongside them he gave a violent start and leapt to his feet.

CHAPTER 21

The evening light faded as the lorry plunged deeper into the hills to the south. In the headlights the rain swung at the windscreen like a steel-beaded curtain. The dirt road was a morass, and the sliding, spinning wheels flung sheets of water into the grass verge. In the cab Cristina urged the lorry forward with every nerve in her body. Its headlights ricocheted off a stone wall, a clump of fig trees, a huddled, drenched cottage. Then the gloomy formless mass of the hills closed round them again.

Cristina glanced at Sabastian. In the twilight his finely chiselled face was drawn and anxious. The irony did not escape her. With his ambition almost achieved he was now terrified the Grotto would cheat him at the last minute and leave him with murder on his soul.

The road grew worse, potholes filled with water appearing in the headlights. Sabastian drove over them recklessly, the lorry bucking and skidding in the mud. On their right the hills fell away as the road looped out towards the cliffs. The wind was stronger here, buffeting the cab windows. Two hundred yards more and they reached the point where the road swung back inland. For a moment Cristina believed Sabastian was going to try to drive the lorry off the road and over the cliff top in a reckless attempt to save time, and she held her breath. Then he shook his head, switched off the engine, and jumped down.

She followed him, her feet sinking into the wet grass. Far below she could hear the sea breaking against the rocks. As she ran round the front of the lorry Sabastian took her arm and shouted over the sound of the wind. 'I shall have to run... Stay here in the lorry until we get back.'

She shook her head fiercely and ran after him. Somehow she managed to keep up with him for over half a mile. Then seeing her distress, he eased his pace and turned to her. Instantly she urged him on. 'Don't waste any time. I'll be all right.'

He hesitated a moment, then ran on. At the top of the last ascent he stopped, a black silhouette against the slate grey sky. She stumbled up after him, half-sick with exhaustion, terrified at what she might see when the cruel face of the cliff of Tiberius came into view. As she neared Sabastian he turned round, his pale face triumphant.

'It hasn't happened yet, *cara*. He is still safe.'

She saw he was right: the dark water swirling at the base of the cliff showed no sign of abnormal disturbance. But the relief that made her tired legs sag was displaced immediately by fear as a gust of wind drove the driving rain into her face. Long minutes must pass before they could climb down the cliff and warn him; the thing still had time to snatch his life away. Her voice struck at Sabastian like a whip. 'What are you waiting here for? He's not safe yet.'

Her words stung him into action again. He started forward, then turned to her. 'Stay on the cliff top, *cara*. Stay here until we get back.'

The need for haste was too great for her to argue with him. They ran across the thick neck of headland to the point where the cliff was eroded. She was thirty yards behind him when he waved a hand and started down. She waited half a minute and then started after him. His startled, angry voice came faintly back over the boom of the wind.

'Go back. Mother of Heaven, do you want to be killed…? Go back and wait on the cliff top.'

'I'll keep well away from the Grotto,' she lied, unable to know whether he could hear her or not. 'I'll stay at the foot of the cliffs.'

For a moment it seemed his anxiety for her would bring him back up the cliff. Then, to her relief, after waving frantically for her to return, he continued his climb downwards.

Slipping and sliding she followed him. Rain was running in sluices down the overhanging rocks and soon she was drenched to the skin. As she climbed down her eyes were fixed on the sea, where every larger wave made her wince with fear.

When she reached the foot of the main cliffs Sabastian was working his way round the headland. He cupped his hands, and although the wind carried his voice away she knew it was a warning to stay back. In spite of the danger she had no intention of obeying – she was too afraid what might happen when he and Michael met in the Grotto – but to avoid any waste of time she paused until he had vanished from sight. Then she started along the headland.

With the rocks treacherous in the rain it was a more difficult climb than she had expected, and it was minutes before she reached the broader shelf of rock that ran downwards to the end of the headland. Here, muddy and drenched, she could make better time, and a few seconds later the Grotto came into sight. There was no sign of either Michael or Sabastian – a fact ominous in itself – only the sinister cave into which the dark sea ebbed and flowed. Instinct warned her time was running out, and yet no sound reached her but the boom of the wind and the rush of the waves. With one terror stumbling over another, she scrambled across the slippery rocks towards the dark entrance.

The scene inside the Grotto checked her. Sabastian, his back to the gully, was held in the beam of the torch like a man with a long arm at his throat. In the nebulous haze behind the light she could just see Michael's muscular, threatening figure. His grim voice came to her over the swish of the water.

'Tell the truth, damn you. Where are your men – waiting at the top of the cliffs?'

The overwrought Italian made a gesture of incredulity. 'Why will you not believe me? I've come to get you out of here before you're killed. Ask Cristina when you see her.'

The torch moved threateningly nearer to Sabastian. 'Where is she? What have you done with her?'

'I keep on telling you – she is at the foot of the cliffs. There is no time to explain now, but it was too dangerous to let her come in here…'

'You're lying, damn you. You heard about the letters her father wrote me and you stopped her coming…'

Cristina had heard enough and ran forward. 'No, Michael. It's all true what he's saying. You are in danger. Terrible danger.'

The torch swung round, blinding her. Michael's voice was suddenly uncertain. 'Tina … I don't understand. Why have you brought Cerone with you?'

The lichen-stained walls of the Grotto reeled dizzily out of the darkness as she pushed the torch aside and seized his arm. 'I'll explain everything later – there's no time now. Come, Michael – quickly...'

His perplexity was like a stubborn rope, holding him against her frantic tugging. 'Why have you brought him with you? What has happened?'

She wanted time, long minutes of it, to explain everything to him. As she hesitated Sabastian answered for her. 'She didn't bring me. I came myself to warn you of the danger.'

The torch swung on him again. 'Warn me! Why should you want to do that?'

The Italian could not hide his triumph. 'Because she promised to marry me if I came. Now are you satisfied?'

The very air seemed to draw in on itself and freeze as Michael stared at him and then at Cristina. When she did not speak he grabbed her shoulder and pulled her roughly round. There was an edge of fear in his voice. 'What's the matter with you? Why don't you deny it?'

'It's true, Michael. I couldn't do anything else but promise...'

He looked as if a sudden fist had leapt out from the darkness and smashed him in the face. 'You've promised to marry him... In

God's name, why?'

'It was the letters, Michael – they didn't come from my father. Maria found everything out and told Sabastian. It was he who wrote the letters – he wrote two because at first he couldn't be certain the rain would last... I discovered what had happened but on my way here he stopped me. When he told me what was going to happen I couldn't do anything else but promise. I couldn't let you die, Michael.'

His snarl was as savage and ominous as that of a wild animal. 'What did he tell you was going to happen?'

She lifted a trembling hand and pointed to the huge hole into which the gully ran. 'That hole isn't shallow but must run right back into the island. Sabastian thinks that somewhere up there it connects with an underground lake. In good weather the lake must dry a little, but after hours of heavy rain it fills and fills until suddenly it spills over and the overflow pours down the conduit.' The reminder of their peril made her voice urgent. 'The conduit must run downhill for miles and miles and the pressure the water builds up must be enormous. That's what makes the screaming noise – the water forces the air before it like a huge whistle... We must get away, Michael...! If the water catches us in here we won't have a chance. Sabastian says it usually takes about eight hours' heavy rain to start it, and the rain began at noon today...'

His harsh voice interrupted her. 'You're not going to keep that promise. It was forced out of you by a trick, by lies. You're under no obligation to keep a promise made that way.' When she did not answer the beam of his torch blinded her. 'Do you hear what I'm saying, Tina?'

She could not speak, but her white, agonised face was an answer in itself. Seeing it he pulled her fiercely towards him. 'Don't you understand why I asked you to meet me here tonight? I was going to ask you to marry me – to settle this devil's persecution once and for all. Now do you understand why you must break it?'

Sabastian was watching her, the black glitter in his eyes both a taunt and warning. She saw it and wished she were dead. 'He made me swear it if he saved you tonight. I can't break a promise like that, Michael.'

'But it was all a trick – it was forced out of you.' When she did not speak he cursed and swung round on the Italian. 'Wasn't it, Cerone – a filthy trick like the rest you've played on her?'

The Italian's voice was soft with hate. 'It was no trick. I wanted to kill you. I never thought of bargaining for your life until she suggested it.'

'You're a liar. You had every move worked

out. All except one,' and as he spoke Michael stepped abruptly between Sabastian and the Grotto entrance. 'You were so confident we'd fall for the trick that you didn't bring any of your thugs with you. That was a mistake, Cerone. We're alone at last, and if Tina won't break her promise you're going to give it back to her or stay here until you do.'

Sabastian stared at him incredulously. 'You're mad. I said it the other day and it is true. You fool, don't you realise that any minute now thousands of tons of water will come raging out of the hole? That it will be like an enormous pressure hose and will smash us all to pulp?'

'That's your story. I don't believe it. But if you're scared give Tina her promise back. Then you can go.'

In spite of the chill in the Grotto there was a glint of sweat on Sabastian's face. 'I'm not lying to you – it's going to happen. If you don't care about your own life, in the name of the Saints, at least get Tina out.'

Michael motioned to Cristina. 'Go and wait on the cliff top. I'll be as quick as I can.'

She drew back. 'I'm not going without you. But we must all go. Michael, I know from the way he told me that he's telling the truth...'

'Then go out and wait.' He reached for her but she ran further back into the Grotto.

'I'm not going, Michael. Not until you come with me.'

He cursed and laid his torch down on the rocks. In the reflected light he looked a menacing figure as he turned to Sabastian. 'In that case the sooner we get this over the better. The promise, Cerone. Give it back to her.'

The Italian's swollen lips drew back, mocked him. 'Do you think anything in the world could make me do that? I said you are mad and you are.'

'We'll find out, Cerone. We'll find out.'

'Get back, you fool. Do you want to be killed?'

For an answer the Italian received a blow in the face that sent him reeling. Growling like an infuriated bulldog Michael went after him, tore two more vicious blows into his body. Sobbing with pain Sabastian dropped on the guano-stained floor of the Grotto. He tried to rise, only for another savage blow to send him sprawling again. Michael stood over him, his face like the granite cliff outside. 'I want that promise back, Cerone. Or get up. Otherwise I'm going to start working you over with my boot.'

With a sudden curse Sabastian tore off his oilskin and thrust his hand inside his jacket. As he leapt to his feet something glinted in the torchlight. Cristina gave a cry of fear.

'Be careful, Michael. He has a knife.'

She ran between them. Sabastian motioned her aside. His handsome face was thinned with fury, as vicious as a spitting cat. 'Get out of my way, *cara*. Quickly – out of my way.'

'I won't. Not until you drop that knife.'

He swore and jerked her aside. Fury gave the act more violence than he intended, throwing her heavily to the ground. As Michael gave a growl and leapt forward the Italian swung round, knife extended. 'Now, Englishman. We'll see who makes the threats now.'

Michael was forced back along the gully. His eyes searched the ground but there were no stones suitable for a weapon. They passed through the white beam of the torch that shone obliquely along the floor of the Grotto. Blood was black on Sabastian's face. He made no sound other than his harsh, purposeful breathing. Michael saw the rear wall of the Grotto was only a few feet behind him and braced himself.

'Tina,' he shouted abruptly. 'The torch. Switch it off.'

She had the presence of mind to understand and react at once. A click and darkness sprang like an animal and blinded them. For a moment there was no sound but the swish of the waves and the booming of the wind. Then came a scuffle, a cry of pain, and the gasping of struggling men.

Torch in hand Cristina listened to the

fighting in an agony of uncertainty. A far-off booming drowned it. At first she believed it only another gust of wind on the headland above, but instead of falling away it grew steadily louder. It was a sound that might have come from the other end of a speaking tube if someone were blowing air into it, and with a sudden thrill of terror she knew what it was.

'Michael … Sabastian … it's started. The water is coming down the tunnel.'

CHAPTER 22

The two men had heard it: their struggles had ceased. Their white faces swam out of the darkness towards her as she switched on the torch. Sabastian was crossing himself. 'Holy Mother, it is coming… Get outside the Grotto as fast as you can and make for the cliff. It's not safe on the headland: the waves can still sweep you away.'

The booming sound was steadily rising in pitch, bringing a fine tremor to the rocks under their feet. With it the draught from the blow-hole began to sharpen, increasing the fetid smell of decay and wet earth that had so long haunted the Grotto. High up in the roof came a startled rustle of wings and the blackness seemed to drop as the swarm of bats made to escape. The light maddened some of them: they flew wildly at the torch. Cristina dropped it with a cry of fear and shrank back against the side wall. Sabastian gripped her arm and dragged her forward. 'Quickly, *carissima*. We've only seconds to get out.'

Bats flew into their faces, half-blinding them as they ran for the entrance. They had barely cleared it before the air in the blow-hole, compressed by the enormous pressure of water behind it, burst through the Grotto in a high-pitched blast of sound. It tore the tops off the nearest waves and sent a sheet of spindrift flying backwards. Fierce eddies of air curled around the side of the Grotto, twisting and tugging the men and the girl like invisible hands and making their escape more difficult.

The differences of Sabastian and Michael were forgotten now as both men united in helping Cristina over the slippery rocks. Sabastian was frantic with fear for her as he urged her on. Somehow, buffeted by the wind and drenched by rain and spray, they managed to round the corner of the headland where the air was calmer. Here the rock-ledge widened, and they were able to scramble madly upwards for twenty yards before reaching a point where it ended in a tangle of black rocks. Sabastian leapt among them and helped Cristina down. She turned her white face to Michael who was behind them. The scream of the wind was rising to a climax now and he had to put his ear to her mouth. 'Hurry, Michael. We must get as far from it as we can...'

Fifteen yards more and they reached a second, narrower ledge. Sabastian jumped on to it and Michael helped Cristina up to him. As he reached for the ledge himself a second noise added itself to the high-pitched scream. It resembled the noise made by an approaching train in a deep subway, an awesome rumble that shuddered the headland. It turned Sabastian's frantic face towards them. His words were lost in the noise but his gestures conveyed their urgency.

They threw themselves madly forward, slipping, bruising themselves against the rough rocks. The scream rose to a final crescendo. Michael caught a shoe between two rocks, stumbled and dropped back a few yards behind the others. Cristina saw him fall and turned white-faced to help him. In turning she slipped herself. She partly steadied herself, but in spite of Sabastian's frantic grab she over-balanced and stumbled off the ledge.

Her hands, catching the ledge as she fell, partly broke her fall and she dropped feet-first on a cluster of huge, seaweed-covered boulders. By dropping flat and clawing at them she somehow managed to avoid sliding down to the waves that swept their base. Before Michael could move a finger to help her Sabastian leapt recklessly down. His feet slipped on the seaweed and he fell with brutal force, but he recovered in an instant and threw a protecting arm around her.

It happened in less time than Michael could cover the six yards that separated them. Answering Sabastian's frantic gestures he lay flat on the ledge, and with the Italian helping to support her, he was able to catch hold of Cristina's hands and draw her up to the ledge alongside him. As he turned back to help Sabastian the wild scream from the Grotto suddenly ceased.

In spite of the massive rumbling that was shaking the cliff it seemed to leave behind it a dense cloud of silence that for a moment stifled their movements. At the same time the sea beneath Sabastian receded. It was a movement eerie in its unnaturalness. The submerged rocks at the base of the boulders reared up, black and dripping. Michael caught a glimpse of wet shingle and sand. In the darkness beyond, the sea appeared to be rising on itself like a terrifying black wall...

He shouted down to the Italian, his voice sounding feeble in his deafened ears. 'Get up, man. Get up and catch hold of my hands!'

Sabastian tried to rise but failed. For the first time Michael realised the Italian had injured himself in his reckless leap to save Cristina. As he swung his legs round to jump down Sabastian's faint, urgent shout reached him. 'No. There's no time. Look after Tina…'

Before Michael could jump all hell broke loose. The sea, recovering from the impact of thousands of tons of water released into it at unimaginable pressure, had reasserted its might again. A black wall of water came lunging out of the darkness like a mountain gone mad. The rocks at the far end of the headland took the first shock and the very cliff seemed to reel. The wave swept on, struck another prominence, and exploded upwards like a depth-charge. The remainder of the wave swept along the side of the headland towards the ledge where Michael and Cristina were crouching.

There was a deep cleft in the back of the ledge a few yards from them. Michael had just time to fling Cristina into it and throw himself over her before the wave reached them.

If it had struck the ledge from the side they could not have survived. As it was the high ledge severed the wave and only its crest swept down on them. Even so it hit them like an avalanche, crushing their bodies down on the rocks. Minutes seemed to pass before its choking weight lifted. Bruised, half-suffocated, they had only seconds to gasp for air before a second wave, smaller than the first but massive enough by any other standards, crushed them again. A few seconds' respite followed, giving them a chance to cough the water from their tortured lungs before a third and last wave swept down the ledge.

When they were at last able to rise and leave the cleft there was no sign of Sabastian. The sea all around the headland was a maelstrom of broken waves and raging water, covering the very boulders on which he had lain.

Neither spoke. Neither could feel much emotion yet: their minds were stunned by the tragedy and the immense powers that had been unleashed around them. As Michael helped Cristina back along the headland the black waves leapt up at them like wolves, trying to add them to the victims of the Grotto.

They saw Sabastian when they reached the foot of the main cliffs, a dark shape huddled high on the rocks where the first great wave had tossed him. Michael wanted Cristina to stay back but she took no notice, hurrying over the rocks as if her very haste could save his life.

He was not drowned as they had expected – the very fury of the wave had given no time for that. But although his face was unmarked by the rocks his body was as broken as a doll that had been hurled against a wall. A faint spark of life remained in him and his eyelids flickered open as they bent over him.

'Sabastian,' Cristina whispered. 'Can you hear me?'

For a long moment his eyes were blank. Then a look of awe drove the opaqueness of death from them. 'Is that you, *carissima?* Are you really alive?'

'Yes, we escaped. 'I'm alive.'

A joy and a relief beyond the telling illuminated his face. 'Ah *Dio*... Thank God for His mercy...'

'Are you in pain?' she whispered.

He tried to shake his head. His eyes were drinking in her face with the frightening thirst of one with only seconds left before the awful sweep into eternity.

'*Carissima,* I'm sorry... Will you believe me?'

Silent grief was racking her body. 'Of course I'll believe you. You saved my life.'

'No, I nearly destroyed it... It was a madness, *carissima*. I loved you too much...'

The life in him was fading fast. Delirium brought the look of an eager, innocent child to his face. 'Let's go to Proccio tomorrow, Tina. Emilio says there are crayfish in the blue cove again. Ask your mother if you can take lunch with you...'

Three minutes later he was dead. She sobbed as Michael put an arm around her drenched shoulders. 'That's what made it so much worse, Michael. He was once my friend.'

'He died your friend, Tina. Always think of it that way.'

He led her gently to the cliff top. As they reached it they saw the distant wink and gleam of torches. She turned to him. 'It could be my father and brother. I've been away a long time and they would guess I came here.'

Habit had made her pull away from him at the nearness of others. Now she remembered her freedom and suddenly the cold and pain left her drenched body. She took Michael's hand again, and with the rain on their faces, erect and close to one another, they waited for the approaching lights.

The publishers hope that this book has given you enjoyable reading. Large Print Books are especially designed to be as easy to see and hold as possible. If you wish a complete list of our books please ask at your local library or write directly to:

Dales Large Print Books
Magna House, Long Preston,
Skipton, North Yorkshire.
BD23 4ND

This Large Print Book, for people
who cannot read normal print,
is published under the auspices of

THE ULVERSCROFT FOUNDATION

... we hope you have enjoyed this book.
Please think for a moment about those
who have worse eyesight than you ...
and are unable to even read or enjoy
Large Print without great difficulty.

You can help them by sending a
donation, large or small, to:

**The Ulverscroft Foundation,
1, The Green, Bradgate Road,
Anstey, Leicestershire, LE7 7FU,
England.**
or request a copy of our brochure for
more details.

The Foundation will use all donations
to assist those people who are visually
impaired and need special attention
with medical research, diagnosis
and treatment.

Thank you very much for your help.